Jesus in America
and other stories from the field

Jesus in America
and other stories from the field

Claudia Gould

Foreword by Lee Haring

Utah State University Press
Logan, Utah

Utah State University Press
Logan, Utah 84322-7800
USUPress.org

Manufactured in the United States of America
Printed on acid-free paper

ISBN 978-0-87421-759-9 (paper)
ISBN 978-0-87421-760-5 (e-book)

Library of Congress Cataloging-in-Publication Data

Gould, Claudia.
 Jesus in America : and other stories from the field / Claudia Gould ;
foreword by Lee Haring.
   p. cm.
 ISBN 978-0-87421-759-9 (pbk. : acid-free paper) – ISBN 978-0-87421-760-5 (e-book)
 1. Religious fiction, American. 2. Parables. 3. Ethnology–Fiction. I. Title.
 PS3607.O884J47 2009
 813'.6–dc22
                          2009034622

Contents

Foreword

Lee Haring

Readers of novels won't let fiction be fiction; they want it to give them fact. The most degrading habit of radio or television interviewers is urging some novelist like Philip Roth to admit that his characters are "really" disguised versions of characters he has known. We first use novels, of course, to find out whether there's anybody else out there, but our second, lifelong use for them is anthropological. Novels and short stories are windows through which we observe other people's "manners, customs, observances, superstitions" (W. J. Thoms's constituents of folklore). Conversely, when readers think, *anthropology should be anthropology*, they mean the writer should conform to a rhetoric they recognize: an encyclopedia-article summary of people's customs, geographic situation, and economic circumstances, followed by extended analyses of kinship relations, preferably in tabular form. When Carlos Castaneda began publishing his series of pseudoanthropological narratives in the 1960s, readers were divided. One set were beguiled by the appropriateness of the teachings of Don Juan to their spiritual needs; the other set, much smaller, said, "Where is the group for whom this character speaks? Where are any tokens of real field experience?" Evidently "the traditional rationalistic and scientistic paradigms" (Kremer 1992, 201) needed just such a challenge as Castaneda posed, to enable a new hybrid to become part of the accepted genre system.

Ethnographic fiction is a phrase rather like *deconstruction*, something people quickly acquire so that they can make their own abusive definition of it, then use it as a weapon against those they don't agree with. They can take a concept or image some professional uses, which the critic thinks is contrived or lacking a real referent, and dismiss it in statements like "culture is itself an ethnographic fiction." Internal to the discipline of anthropology is the equally contemptuous use of the phrase to mean something formerly

1

accepted by professionals, but now exploded, like the supposed ignorance of non-Western people about where babies come from.

That is not the ethnographic fiction in this book. Seen more correctly, ethnographic fiction is a technique for recasting field notes. An author uses the familiar rhetoric of the short story or novel as a means of palatably conveying what was discovered in the field. The classic example, assigned to many anthropology students before the genre got its name, is *Return to Laughter*, Laura Bohannan's novel about the Tiv in Nigeria. For it she adopted the pseudonym Elenore Smith Bowen, so that no colleague, dean, or student would think she was offering such an engaging, well-written fiction as "real" ethnography. But "real" field experience lay behind it, as it does behind the stories in this book. Then instructors began assigning Chinua Achebe's *Things Fall Apart*, whose author, in an admirable exposé of cultural convergence, quite deliberately addressed readers with information about Igbo culture. Once instructors had become accustomed to this generic boundary-crossing, they were able to perceive Zora Neale Hurston as its pioneer. Whereas Hurston obliges her reader to notice how involved she is with her informants, Claudia Gould limits her visibility. In a partly autobiographical Afterword, she reveals that these are "her people," in the precise sense of that phrase that they would understand: her relatives and their neighbors in Morganton, North Carolina. In fact, her choice to write fiction, rather than a monograph on "the place of Protestant Christianity in the lives of North Carolinians," manifests her dedication to her extended family and others. She makes the difficult decision not to write "straight" ethnography, because she can bring more of herself to serve them through writing fiction.

But hasn't fiction always been ethnographic? What is *Robinson Crusoe* if not a study in unaccommodated man, recreating a class-based society? Balzac consigned an entire writing life to his ethnography of the emerging Paris bourgeoisie, initially calling it "Studies of Customs." Flaubert proclaimed himself an ethnographer of Rouen in his subtitle *Scenes of Provincial Life*. To update Balzac, whilst narrowing the population being studied (in harmony with contemporary anthropological trends), became the mission of Marcel Proust in the Faubourg Saint-Antoine. Among British novelists (Fielding and Trollope leap to mind as reporters from the provinces), the most outspoken ethnographer is Dickens, whose Mr. and Mrs. Veneering "were bran-new people in a bran-new house in a bran-new quarter of London. Everything about the Veneerings was spick and span new. All their furniture was new, all their friends were new, all their servants were new, their plate was new, their carriage was new, their harness was new, their horses were new, their pictures were new, they themselves were new . . . ." Thomas Hardy soon explained the method: "Under the general name of 'Egdon Heath,' which has been given to the sombre scene of the story [*The Return of the Native*], are united or typified heaths of various real names . . . ." It's commonplace for readers now to look for and find the precise geography in *Ulysses*, the intellectual history in *The Mandarins*, the ferocious sociology in *Main Street*, and the nostalgic biographical-literary history in *A Moveable Feast*. Claudia Gould, insisting by her example that realistic fictions are a legitimate genre of scientific writing, expands the concept of ethnographic fiction.

In "A Red Crayon," for example, the images of hellfire and brimstone purveyed in church are not merely a metonym for child-beating, which the community's values accept as a legitimate part of the duty of a churchgoing father. The images are themselves the abuse, in both this story and "Jack at the Mercy Seat." The girl (the narrator as child) who has borrowed a crayon from Sunday school comes to feel like "the biggest sinner in the world." But the author does not oversimplify. Abusive childrearing in these two dimensions isn't accepted by everyone in the community. Neither the girl's mother nor her Sunday school teacher participates in the girl's self-condemnation; the mother takes the child out of Sunday school, and ever after, the narrator has stayed away from church. This is a divided community, then, even in the religion its members think is their truest basis for unity.

Expanding the discipline of anthropology by incorporating social criticism, psychology, and sociology of religion with her own self-fashioning, Claudia Gould firmly situates herself as a creative writer who works from ethnographic and autobiographical materials. As part of her expanding program, she addresses the old belief that to tell a story must mean some sort of resistance to ethnographic reality. Now that narrativity has become a viable, indeed central term in much criticism (Ricoeur 1985; Greimas 1970, 1983; Herman 1999), the chink in the wall is growing larger. Through her pieces, she contends that the familiar short-story style, without postmodern derangements of time or switchings of point of view, will evoke the reader's traditional expectation, based on realism, that here's a way to find out what these people are like. Her method calls up the feature of her subjects that people most often expect from folklore, an orientation to the past. "Personal Storage," for instance, portrays a woman who can't be distracted by financial troubles from her attachment to her old furniture and family papers. Where her treasure is, there is her heart also (Matthew 6:21). The reader, identifying with the Farm Home Administration worker who passes on her story, is as appalled as he is; conflicts of value, we see, are part of the manners and customs of this population. Claudia Gould invents a monologue that captures the social reality of this imagined character's attachment to the past, a character who is not a folksinger, storyteller, or quilter, but no less a product of Southern culture.

The author reveals the past orientation of her people most clearly, through the story "Jack at the Mercy Seat," when she crosses her own boundary, reproducing in her Afterword the spoken words of the original of her character Jack. That is, only at the end of her book does she supply the quotation that would be the main component of a conventional folkloric account. Starting backward from that testimony, Jack's whole life is seen in retrospect, back to his early church experiences. Then, in wartime, the images of hellfire from those days come back to him. A superhuman visitation from a devil-like figure leads him through fear to salvation, a step which takes him down the path of imagining his wife's adultery, abusing her physically, being rejected by her, and supposing he can patch it up. Drunkenness, his own adultery, shiftlessness, fighting, drifting, and apparent bigamy bring him in the end to church. His story stops before he gives testimony.

The author's sociological statement here about southern Protestant Christianity is so strong that a reader might miss the folkloric elements: the fantasy about kamikaze pilots, the ethnic slur ("the Japs were crazy"), or the folk-speech word *mistake* for an unplanned child. Framing Jack's life retrospectively is a sufficiently complicated device to do him and his people justice. Claudia Gould's response to the intractable complexity of church culture in North Carolina is to show in fiction the varieties of pressure the past exerts on her people's present. An obvious goal of her stories is to affirm the central role of Protestant religion in American life, but the sociology serves the fiction.

Part of the complication she engages is the question a reader can get distracted from, "Who is speaking?" Ruth, in "The Mountains of Spices," speaks for herself; we don't know whether she speaks for her author. Claudia Gould captures here a moment in Southern Christian history when an independent daughter could internalize

Scripture in a way the previous generation didn't practice (for example, Scripture doesn't touch the families' racism). The author captures that moment through a generational conflict. Gender, race, and class have placed Ruth in a situation she escapes by making Scripture real for herself, regarding herself as worthy to make her own plans, and being willing to pay the price of departing from the "family values" of two families. Thus she contributes to the fragmentation of an American family, resigning herself to repeating what is, after all, the most ancient American pattern, uprooting and resettling elsewhere. Thus she speaks for a new, personalized Christianity, while her author enacts the notion of "intersectionality" in the converging effects of religion, gender, and class.

The recent past of American folklore studies has been blessed with many innovative contributions by female scholars (Kapchan 1993; Magliocco 2004; Turner 2009; Lawless 1988; Lawless 1993). An especially successful nonfictional alternative to Claudia Gould's ethnographic fiction is Margaret K. Brady's *Mormon Healer and Folk Poet*, in which, out of scraps of information and by demonstrating the interdisciplinary character of folklore, the author creates a completed portrait of a classic folkloric character, a nobody who becomes somebody through Brady's research (Brady 2009). Closer to these short stories, in the sort of fieldwork involved, is a notable study by Margaret Yocom of members of her family. Amongst them she finds a "private sphere of women's personal experience narratives" as "a mode of social interaction, a space where none need fear ridicule or embarrassment" (Yocom 1985, 52). These authors exemplify the attraction felt in folklore studies for what might be called "submerged populations"–which is the phrase the great Frank O'Connor used to point to the invisible characters that the short-story genre prefers. Such are the characters explored and created by Claudia Gould, in Laurel ("A Moment of Rapture") and in Ruth and her mother ("The Mountains of Spices"). She does not ignore the inescapable awkwardness of male-female interaction, for instance when the Farm Home Administration man in "Personal Storage" has to reproduce the story of a woman he can't hope to understand deeply, as if he were a folklorist without knowing it.

In-between spaces are familiar, in a world where cultures continually converge and expectations are continually surprised. Claudia Gould's reader comfortably occupies such a space.

Bibliography

Brady, Margaret K. *Mormon Healer and Folk Poet: Mary Susannah Fowler's Life of "Unselfish Usefulness"*. Logan: Utah State University Press, 2009.

Greimas, Algirdas Julien. *Du sens; essais sémiotiques*. Paris: Editions du Seuil, 1970.

Herman, David, ed. *Narratologies: New Perspectives on Narrative Analysis*. Columbus: Ohio State University Press, 1999.

Kapchan, Deborah A. *Gender on the Market: Moroccan Women and the Revoicing of Tradition*. Philadelphia: University of Pennsylvania Press, 1993.

Kremer, Jürgen W. "Lifework Carlos Castaneda." *Re-Vision* 14 (1992): 195–203.

Lawless, Elaine J. *Handmaidens of the Lord: Pentecostal Women Preachers and Traditional Religion*. Publications of the American Folklore Society., vol. 9. Philadelphia: University of Pennsylvania Press, 1988.

———. *Holy Women, Wholly Women: Sharing Ministries of Wholeness Through Life Stories and Reciprocal Ethnography*. Publications of the American Folklore Society. New Series. Philadelphia: University of Pennsylvania Press, 1993.

Magliocco, Sabina. *Witching Culture: Folklore and Neo-Paganism in America*. Contemporary Ethnography. Philadelphia, Pa.: University of Pennsylvania Press, 2004.

Ricoeur, Paul. *Time and Narrative*. Vol. 2. Translated by Kathleen McLaughlin and David Pellauer. Chicago: University of Chicago Press, 1985.

Turner, Patricia A. *Crafted Lives: Stories and Studies of African American Quilters*. With a foreword by Kyra E. Hicks. Jackson: University Press of Mississippi, 2009.

Yocom, Margaret R. "Woman to Woman: Fieldwork and the Private Sphere." In *Women's Folklore, Women's Culture*, edited by Rosan A. Jordan and Susan J. Kalčik, 45–53. Philadelphia: University of Pennsylvania Press, 1985.

Jesus in America

Wist ye not that I must be about my Father's business?
—Luke 2:49

Jesse lived with his mother and his father took an interest. Or that's what his mother said. "He cain't be here all the time, honey, but he takes an interest." When Jesse was little, he used to wish that he took more of an interest. He saw his father sometimes. "He never just high-tailed it out, like some men would 'a done." No, Dan, Jesse's father, turned up every so often at the door, and he always seemed real glad to see them, and usually he brought a present. Some kind of a present.

But… What Jesse used to wish when he was little was that he turned up sometimes on the right days. Jesse couldn't remember him ever being there at Christmas, though his mama told him that he was there for Jesse's first one—"and he was just so proud of you!" Jesse asked about that Christmas a lot when he was little, whether it snowed and if they'd had a big tree that stood on the floor instead of a little one you sat on the table, like they always had nowadays. And who else was there—"Did Grandma come?" And whether he could sit up at the table and chew his Christmas dinner already or if somebody had to hold him in his lap and feed him soft stuff with a spoon. He wanted to be able to make a picture in his mind of what it was like, that first Christmas, when he was a little baby. If he could make a good enough picture, he would be able to remember it. Sometimes he thought he did, but then he'd think he was just remembering the picture in his mind. So that was hard.

And he'd never turned up on Jesse's birthday. Not even the first one, the day Jesse was born. "Some men do like to get themselves kindly out of the way for that occasion," Mama explained. That made Grandma laugh, but Jesse couldn't see what was funny about it. And then by the time he was one year old, Dan wasn't there anymore. He had started just taking an interest. When Jesse was little, he used to expect his Daddy would surprise him one birthday and open the back door just in time to see him blow his candles out. He watched for him, holding his breath for the candles, but holding his breath waiting, too. He never said, because Mama worked hard so he could have a nice birthday every year. And Dan did bring him a present whenever he came. So it was no use to make a fuss. It was just a picture in his mind, like his first Christmas, which had really happened, even if he couldn't remember it.

Now that he was twelve, it seemed to him like he'd spent a long time wishing that Dan was around. Sometimes, even now, when he knew it wasn't going to happen, he'd wish his father would be there to watch him play baseball at Shepherd's Field, because he'd started to be a real good pitcher. It surprised everybody, but he had. Mama came when she could, and Grandma almost always came, unless she was working. And it wasn't as if he was the only boy who didn't have a dad there to watch. Heck, Mama was right about that. Two or three of his friends' dads had just high-tailed it out of there. And one of them had died. In the war, Doodle said. "What war? There hasn't been any war since history." But Doodle just said, "You don't know ever'thin'," and Jesse didn't ask him about it anymore because he looked so mournful. Some of them kept trying to make Doodle talk about it, but Jesse thought it was probably bad enough to have your dad dead without having to explain it to everybody all the time. Hell, maybe there had been a war and he just hadn't heard about it.

Jesse missed his dad, but he wasn't lonesome. He had plenty of friends, and he sort of had a girl friend. Her name was Lois and she didn't go to his school, but she lived on his road. They never said they were going around together, but they usually met on the way back from school and they'd shared a couple of cigarettes Lois had got off her older brother. Once she had a marijuana one. She wouldn't say where she got it from, but she let him have a toke. He didn't like it much, but he guessed he'd get used to it when he was older. Like a lot of things. There was a lot of pot around. And stronger things, he guessed, if he'd been trying to get ahold of it. But he wasn't. Grandma would have a fit, for one thing. She'd have a fit just about the cigarettes. She was real strict. He thought Mama had done some drugs when she was young, and that made Grandma more strict with him. Mama wouldn't say, and he didn't like to ask Grandma. Some people said pot was better for you than tobacco, besides being easier to grow. Jesse wasn't too interested. He reckoned the time he'd tried it with Lois he might as well have been smoking shredded lettuce like little kids did. But it was the only time she'd let him kiss her—a real, sexy kiss with both their mouths open. That was actually kind of disappointing, to tell you the truth. He was more thrilled that she'd let him do it than the way it felt. And then she'd started laughing and then he had, too, and they'd smoked up the rest of the thin joint, forgetting to hold the smoke in, the way you're supposed to, passing it back and forth as fast as they could until finally it dropped in the grass and neither of them felt like trying to pick it up, they were laughing too much. There was only enough left to pinch between your fingers anyway. "Never mind," said Lois, "we can easy get some more." But they never did, so far.

He'd got into trouble at school. Not because of the pot. Nobody knew about that except for the boys he'd told. Not because of anything he'd done, really. Not because of bad behavior. Only daydreaming, Mrs. Teniers said, though he didn't remember daydreaming. He did look out the window a lot, it got so boring. And the homework he didn't do. And, he guessed, lying to Mrs. Teniers about why he hadn't done it, and lying to Mama about not having any. That was worst. And not going to school at all. And leaving in the middle of the morning. You had to lie to get away, unless you slipped out when the corridors were pretty busy. And the next day when you had to give an excuse. So it was bad behavior in a way. You could say. But not fighting or anything, or stealing. Or carrying firearms. There was a sign at Reception that said, "No Firearms Of Any Kind To Be Brought Onto School Premises." Jesse thought it made sense, especially after Columbine, but Mama almost screamed the first time she saw it. "I thought it was pretty rough when I was at school," she said, "but at least we never needed a sign like that."

It had been rough, too, when his Mama was at school. She'd told him stories about it. She had to get used to having black people in the same school, for one thing. They didn't used to be allowed. And they got some real tough backwoods white kids, too, down from the mountains. "But we never did have guns. And if the coloreds had knives they kept them to themselves." She hadn't liked school much more than Jesse did, Grandma said. One time she'd started to tell him about when Mama was his age and she was sneakin' off school, but Mama came in and said, "Oh Mom, don't tell him all that stuff. It'll make him think it's all right." Which it didn't, of course. He did it, but he knew it was wrong. It didn't exactly say about sneakin' off school in the Bible, but he guessed that bearing false witness was the same as lying. That's why you had to swear on the Bible when you were a witness in court. And there was honoring your father and your mother, too. Which you weren't doing if you were pretending to go to school and then hanging around town until it was time to go home.

He'd never killed anybody, or even any animals. It wasn't a sin to kill animals. Isaac in the Old Testament liked meat better than vegetables, and so did God. That was what made Cain so mad at Abel. But Jess never even managed to trap a coon when his Uncle Eddie had taken him and his friend Duane coon hunting. He'd liked being out in the moonshine, though, with Duane and Uncle Eddie, staying up all night with the dogs. He called him Uncle, but he was really Grandma's brother and that made him his Great Uncle. There were some commandments he didn't perfectly understand, like having other gods. He guessed that was really aimed at Chinese people and Arabs, people like that. Adultery, of course, you couldn't do until you got married. It's funny there wasn't anything about sexual intercourse in the commandments, because that was a big sin. Maybe it was covered by something else, like lying and false witnessing. But stealing. He was uneasy about stealing. He never had stole much. It never seemed really bad if he only took something like a candy bar and ate it right away or something like that. But the Bible said just not to steal. At all. And it was a kind of stealing, he guessed, even a candy bar. You could call it.

He would be able to put all that badness behind him now, though. He was going to the Christian school. He didn't have to. They would have had him back at the public junior high. They said he was smart enough. Only…they always said it at the same time as they were saying he was bad. "It isn't even as though you were stupid, Jesse." Which made it sound as though it would be better if he was. They would have had him back; they wrote out a contract and he had to agree to it, and he had a book that he had to get signed every day, once at home and once at school. They'd sign it at school if he stayed there all day and Mama had to sign it if he did homework every night. Mrs. Teniers had to write in it what his homework was every day and he had to show it to Mama so she'd know. And there was some more stuff. He was going to have to repeat some subjects, not with Mrs. Teniers but with Mr. Mull, who taught fifth grade. That was because he had missed so much. That part hadn't sounded like a bad idea to him, because he couldn't hardly keep up with sixth grade math, but the principal said, "Now I know it will be a humiliation for you, Jesse, but you have only yourself to blame. And it isn't as though you were stupid." So then he knew he was supposed to feel bad. But you had to expect to get punished if you'd done wrong. He knew that much.

But it turned out he wouldn't have to do any of that because he was going to the Christian school. Mama said that he needed the discipline and Grandma said she'd help all she could with the fees. It made him ashamed because he knew neither of them had much money. He promised he would be good in the public school, but Mama said not to worry, it was for the best and she'd wanted him to go to the Christian school since he was six years old, but she didn't think she could afford it. "Sometimes God just does find a way to tell you what you can afford and what you can't," she said. And then she told him that it wasn't just the discipline, it was the teaching. The public schools were ungodly; they taught that evolution was true—Jesse hadn't got to that yet, or maybe it was one of the things he'd missed—and that it was all right to be queer, and plus the Federal Government had made it a crime to pray in school. And there were people trying to sell you drugs all the time. Jesse didn't know so much about trying to, because the older kids were always complaining about not being able to find any. But then they usually did find some, so he guessed she was right in a way. And everybody cussed. Well, that was pretty true. He was trying not to now, but before, it had been hard not to say bad words—really bad words—in front of Mama, because he got so used to saying them. Now he said "sexual intercourse" instead of "fucking." If he was talking about doing it. He didn't say neither one in front of Mama. If it was like, whose fucking fault is it, then he'd just have to leave it out. Mr. Daniels said things like "get out of the blithering way," and "what's the drooling idea," and he also said, if somebody made him really mad, "Why don't you just go and dump yourself?" which made everybody laugh, but you couldn't say that yourself. You'd just have to leave it out. When he was younger, and didn't completely understand, he'd heard Grandma say, "bang," to mean doing it. It made him laugh out loud, which was too bad because Mama and Grandma noticed he was still there and they'd kind of forgotten until then. Grandma and Mama and Aunt Alice was talking, and Grandma said something like, "They was always ready for a bang," and that was when he laughed. "It sounds like a firecracker," he said, and Grandma said, "Well, honey, if it's good, it is," and they all laughed, but Mama said, "Mama, hush up," and they sent him to bed. In the handbook for his new school it said that they mustn't use any vulgar language or there would be Disciplinary Action.

Mama said she wanted him to grow up to be a good Christian man, and that was more important, she said, even than a good education. Of course the Christian school had high academic standards, too. Not everybody who wanted to could get in. Even if you were able to pay the tuition. Jesse had to be interviewed, when the principal and the pastor mostly asked him about God and Jesus, and then he had to go to school for a day so that they could see what his behavior was like. And he had to have a letter from Reverend Finkle, the pastor at Mount Calvary, to say he and his family were faithful attenders. Even when Mama got the letter to say he'd gotten in, it was on probation. That wasn't anything against him; it was everybody they accepted. Attending Christ the King was a privilege and not a right. You could only stay there if you were willing to make the most of the opportunity.

It was called The School of The Church of Christ the King, but you didn't have to belong to The Church of Christ the King to go there. Him and Mama were going to keep going to Mount Calvary. He was glad about that because church was one of the places he felt happy. He never complained about going to church, and he never sneaked off. The preaching was boring sometimes, but the Sunday school was usually pretty interesting. They had to remember things, but they never had any tests. "All you really need to remember," Miss Gordon, the Sunday school teacher said, "is that Jesus loves you."

†

Jesse had to start the Christian school in the middle of the spring semester, because that's when he got suspended from junior high. He was a little nervous about being new when it wasn't even the beginning of the year. There wouldn't be any other new kids, so he'd get more attention than he really wanted. Mama said it wouldn't matter because it wasn't like the public school; nobody bullied you or tried to make you feel embarrassed.

Everything was different. Grandma bought him new pants, not too tight, it said in the letter, and not too baggy. You weren't allowed to wear jeans. Or baseball caps. Or T-shirts. Grandma bought him new shirts. You had to button your shirt all but the top button, and you had to have it tucked in your trousers. And you had to wear a belt. His regular haircut was all right; neat and short all round. Grandma gave him a trim the night before he started.

Everybody was kind to him. They'd assigned another boy in his class to take him round and tell him things and make sure he was all right. This boy—Daniel, the same as Jesse's dad—was a member of the church, so he knew everything about the church and the school both; he'd been going there since preschool. Daniel said, "You can ask me anything. Don't be bashful." And Jesse had a lot of questions. In a way it wasn't really his first day, because of the day he went for them to judge him, but it felt like the first day. The time before, he'd been too nervous, trying not to look as though he was noticing them watching him, and trying to be completely good. He was still nervous, but he wasn't quite so bad. He didn't think he could do anything bad enough for them to kick him out the first day. Daniel introduced him to a lot of other boys. No girls. There were girls there, but he didn't meet them. Daniel said they were allowed to talk to them, "Of course! People have some weird ideas about what goes on here—brainwashing and everything," but they just didn't happen to. They weren't allowed to touch them, "Of course, if you bump into somebody, you won't get in trouble, or if you have to tap somebody on the shoulder. But you can't hold hands or anything like that." At his old school, girls and boys walked through the corridors together, arms round each other's waists or shoulders. Jesse didn't know whether he was sorry or not to lose the chance of doing that when he was older. He saw one black boy, but Daniel didn't introduce him. He was a little boy, so he didn't need to. Jesse was surprised there weren't more, because the handbook said, "We do not discriminate on the basis of race, or national or ethnic origin." That meant colored. He said to Daniel, "Are there lots of colored here?" and Daniel said, "No." Jesse waited, but he didn't say any more.

†

By the time he came back in the fall—the end of summer, really, because they had a longer year than the public schools—he wasn't the newest any more. He wasn't assigned to take any of the new boys around, but he knew his own way.

They had a Bible Study class every day, and every morning they met in the chapel for a service. And on some afternoons. They had the Lord's Supper, too. But the chapel was always open; they could always go in to pray. That was different from the public schools, where you weren't allowed to pray.

The chapel was very plain. Pastor Happold told them about the grand churches that Catholics had, and synagogues, of course, where Jews went on Saturdays to pray. They were fancy, with gold and marble, because people like that, who had false gods, put the things of the body before the things of the spirit. Theirs, the Chapel of Christ the King, had a tiled floor with a rug on it and all the benches were wooden and the walls were painted white. It had plain glass windows to let in God's light. At first Jesse thought they must not be able to afford stained glass windows like they had at Mount Calvary, but Pastor Happold explained one time about how man was allowed to create beauty—"Serve God in all things!"—but he couldn't improve on what God had made. So the light of the world—just like, he said, the real Light of the World, who was Jesus—didn't need to be colored or poured through a filter. That was the same as trying to take the Bible and make it mean something besides what it said. The pure light was like the pure gospel. And the gospel was the word of God.

At Catawba Junior High School, you could sign up for scripture class as one of your electives, but here it was different. There was scripture in everything. In science and history and English composition. That was because it was God's world and Christ was the king of everything, not just church. God was the god of basketball, Pastor Happold said, just as much as He was god of heaven. Pastor Happold said that the whole world was shining with the presence of God, if only we knew how to look. One of the boys in his class lifted his hand to his head and made screwy circles with his pointing-finger. Jesse looked around, sick with anxiety that their teacher would see Tom, but she was looking at Pastor Happold and not at them. "But," he thought, "God has seen him," and he felt cold with what was in store for Tom. Jesse was surprised that anybody laughed at the pastor. In his old school, everybody made fun of the teachers, and did imitations of them, sometimes while they were right in front of you, with their backs turned, and then they'd stop the second the teacher turned round, which was the funniest of all. Sometimes you couldn't help but laugh. But here…it was almost like laughing at God. Besides, it said in the handbook, "Ridicule of the Christian teachings and ideas presented will not be tolerated."

The fact was that he didn't always get it. Mama was right that nobody bullied you, but that didn't mean they didn't laugh at things you hadn't heard or didn't exactly understand. Maybe he was still too new.

On the Saturday after Thanksgiving, Dan turned up. Jesse knew him from the shape of his face and his hat through the truck window. He was driving a little blue truck that Jesse hadn't seen before.

It looked almost new. Jesse ran out of Grandma's back door—they were staying at Grandma's house—and out onto the dirt driveway before he'd even stopped.

"Hey, Dad," mindful that he wasn't a little boy. Nobody was going to swing him up in his arms now.

"Hey, Son. I declare you've grown a foot! What's she feedin' you, tomater fertilizer?"

He took his father's hand and led him up the steps onto the porch. "We got some coffee," he said. "Mama and Grandma's both at work. You want to go see Mama?"

"Sure do." Dan sat down at the kitchen table. "That coffee hot?"

"I'll pour you some." His heart was hitting his chest. He had only just got here and already Jesse was trying not to ask him how long he was going to stay. "You want Carnation in it?"

"Just sugar," he said.

Jesse put the sugar jar out, and a spoon for stirring. He sat down in a chair across from his dad.

"Ain't you havin' no coffee?"

He shook his head and made a face. "Don't like it," he said. "Hit's too bitter."

Dad laughed. "You like tea?"

"Sweet tea, I do. Ice tea."

"And I bet you like that good ol' rye whisky."

Jesse laughed and shook his head.

"Not yet, huh. Not yet. Well, it'll come. Hell, Jesse, you're nearly a man now. There's all kinds of things you got to develop a taste for."

Jesse laughed again and then he said, "I'm a-goin' to a new school now."

"Is that right? How come you're doin' that?"

"Mama says I need the discipline. And the teachin's better."

"Is that right? How come you need all that discipline? You been in trouble?"

"Not really. Not bad trouble. I was sneakin' off school a little."

His dad laughed. "Just a little, huh. I bet. Do they whup you in that new school?"

Jesse shook his head. "They do, but I ain't got whupped yet. I ain't been bad enough yet."

"How bad you got to be?"

Jesse shrugged. "Pretty bad, I guess. Usin' vulgar language or bein' disobedient."

"Well, you got it in you, boy, I believe that. If you got any a' me in you." He slid his empty cup across the oilcloth-covered table to Jesse. "You go put that in the sink for me and we'll go round to the store and get your mama."

Jesse put the cup under the spigot, ran it full of water and carefully turned the water off before he ran to catch up with his father. He took the key from above the door frame and pulled the door closed behind him.

"You scairt a' burglars?" Dan asked.

"Better safe than sorry, Grandma says."

"I bet she does, too."

"Are we gonna go get Grandma, too? She's nearly done workin'." He climbed up into the passenger seat and stroked the upholstery. "I sure do like your new truck."

"Well, it ain't a real truck, you know, you couldn't haul nothin' much in it. Just a kind of a materiel-carrier." He winked at Jesse as he settled himself behind the wheel. "She still at the same place?" he asked as he turned out into the road.

"Yeah. She likes it there. She says they're real understandin' when she has to take time off or somethin'."

"She got herself some ol' boy she's seein' up to that store?"

Jesse laughed. "No sir, not Mama. She says when you're away I'm the only boy she's got."

"Well, I'm glad to hear it."

They drove past a straggle of houses and fields and along the straight road that led into the town. "Grandma's at the Oxford plant, if you want to go down that way," said Jesse.

"Well now, I guess we'll leave your grandma alone this afternoon and not disturb her arrangements. I'll see her when she gets back home this evenin'." Dan drove in silence until the first traffic light stopped them, then he said, "How come you was home today? I would 'a thought you'd be out playin' or raisin' hell or somethin' on a Saturday."

Jesse laughed. He liked the way his dad talked about him, as though they were the same. "I been out a while, but I came on home when it started to get cold."

"Ain't your friends got houses?" They stopped in front of the Family Dollar store and Dan turned the engine off and started to get out. Jesse followed him, scrambling down the high step and slamming the door as he ran.

Mama had already seen them through the glass and she was

walking toward them when they got to the door. "Well, God help us all," she said, "if he isn't here again!"

Jesse hugged her waist, exuberant, and Dad leaned across him to kiss her. Jesse was still just short enough so he could do that.

"I'm s'posed to be workin', you know," she said, and pulled away from them both. She was turning to walk to the back of the store, but Jesse could hear that she was smiling.

"Well now, Babe," Dan said, "cain't you just have a little time off on account of it's a special occasion?"

"It is a special occasion, I believe, when you show your face around here," she said, but she didn't sound mad.

He leaned on the counter. "Now don't go haulin' up all my sins of yesteryear," he said, and his wife laughed.

"Yesteryear!" she said, "It just keeps on bein' yesteryear if that's when you do your sinnin'."

"You're a hard woman, Edith," he said.

"Well, I guess I am," she said. "I need to be, what I have to put up with."

"Come on, now," he said, "ain't it time we had a little family life?"

"I'd be ashamed, if I was you," she said. "It's nearly time I was quittin' anyway. You can just hang around and wait for me if you want to." She gestured widely to the tables of shirts and underwear, lengths of cloth, children's shoes and knick-knacks. "You can do some shoppin'."

Dan began to walk methodically through the aisles, picking up cellophane-wrapped objects and scrutinizing them as though he couldn't make them out. Jesse followed him, trying not to laugh. There was a high stack of dishtowels and Dan started sorting through them as though he were looking for a particular design. Finally he held up one that was printed with a calendar for 1998 under a picture of Christ in a garden, his hand raised as though in blessing, his sandaled feet set on the 1 and the second 9. "Now here," he said. "This is real nice. I think I better buy this for your grandma. You think she'd notice it's a little out of date? I reckon I should get a little discount, don't you? Seein' it's past its sell-by."

Jesse laughed, but he felt scandalized, too. He had a feeling that his father was making fun of Grandma and of Jesus at the same time. He was glad they were too far away from Mama for her to hear him.

When they were ready to leave, everybody said goodbye to Dan and Mr. Randolph said it sure was nice to see him again. Jesse was glad everybody was so friendly, but when they got outside, Dan said,

"He seems pretty familiar, just to be your boss."

Mama looked at him and shook her head. "You know you're as crazy as a coot, don't you?" They had been walking toward the new blue truck, and she turned to Jesse, "You ridin' home with your daddy, or you want to come with me?"

"I'll ride with Daddy, please," he said, "if that's all right."

"Sure is." She looked at the truck. "That's pretty," she said.

"It was a bargain. Fact, it was almost a present. Fella owed me some money."

"Well, there's a first," she said.

†

When Grandma walked in, she looked at Dan and said, "I thought it was you with that truck."

"Classy," he agreed.

She shook her head. "Bumper sticker."

Jesse ran outside to look. He hadn't actually stood behind the truck yet. It said, "Country Music's My Religion and Hank Williams is My God." He felt a little worried by it, although he knew it was only a joke. He guessed he couldn't come to pick him up from school Monday after all, if he was still here Monday.

They all went out to eat together, Grandma too, at the Moondance Fish Camp. They had the all-you-can-eat special and Jesse had three platefuls. Then when they got home, Dan tried to get Edith to go out dancing at Cat Square, but she wouldn't. "Come on, Sweetness," he said. "Gloria don't mind keepin' an eye on Jesse, do you Gloria?"

Grandma said no, she didn't mind a bit, but Edith said that Cat Square was a dive and she was a married woman, "though you wouldn't know it."

"But honey, you got married way too young. You never would 'a done if it hadn't 'a been for..." an inclination of his head. "You're just a young thing at heart. You better get you some fun while you got the chanst. Before you got a whole bunch more kids."

"You better not start countin' 'em," she said.

They did go out together after Jesse was in bed, walking off down the road because Mama said she wasn't getting in the car with him if he was going to be drinking. Jesse stood at the window and watched them walk in and out of the tree shadows that lay across the road, his mom's pale coat appearing and vanishing.

Then he went to bed. When his dad was away, Jesse always prayed that he'd come back and when he was home, he always prayed that he'd stay.

Dan didn't wake up in time for church on Sunday, and when they got home he was out of bed, but he was still drunk. Jesse heard Grandma say, "I believe he's got hold of some liquor already today. Did he bring some back last night?"

Edith shrugged. "I didn't see any," she said.

"It beats me how he pays for it," said Grandma.

He couldn't eat dinner with them, but in the afternoon he was better and he took Jesse for a walk down the creek. Grandma said how could Mama trust him with that boy, but Mama said Jesse would always be safe with his daddy. Jesse wasn't ever worried about being with Dan unless he was awful drunk, and he was fine now.

"You got school again tomorrow?"

Jesse nodded.

"They don't give you much time off at that school, do they?"

"No sir, they don't. And they'll keep you late if you have to wait for somebody to come get you, on account a' work or somethin'."

"It's a Christian school, right?"

"Christ the King," Jesse said.

"You like that? All that church and Jesus and Bible all day?"

He shrugged. "I guess." Then he remembered Columbine and Cassie Bernall and he said, "Yes, I do."

"Well," his father said, "just as long as you like it."

They walked along together for a while, crossing back and forth across the road so as to stay in the sun, which was getting low and red in the sky.

"It's hard, ain't it," Dan said, "livin' with women."

Jesse had never thought about it. "It ain't hard to live with Mama," he said. And then, feeling disloyal, he added, "or Grandma, neither."

"Well, that's good," his father said. "That's real good. The longer you stay a boy the better you'll do, I believe."

Jesse wished he could take it back. He'd rather be a man for his father, a friend. But he hadn't got it in time. And Mama and Grandma were always there, but Dad... So maybe that was right. Maybe he was a boy.

Dan didn't get drunk again, not that Jesse saw, and he guessed he would have. He came and picked him up at school and nobody saw the bumper sticker. Or nobody said.

He had supper with them every night, and he and Mama talked about moving back to their own house. "It wouldn't take me two weeks to get that insulation finished," he said, "if I can get some help. We could be back there before Christmas."

"We could have Christmas dinner," said Jesse. "Grandma could come."

"She sure as hell could," said Dan, and he squeezed Jesse's shoulders. "We'll get us one of those big ol' sugar-cured hams from down the country."

Dan took the keys to the house and went over there with fat rolls of pink fiberglass. When Jesse asked if he could help, he said, "I'm relyin' on you!" He said he'd get Jesse some thick gloves and a breathing mask because you have to treat fiberglass with respect. Jesse went up to his old room while Dad was looking at the walls he'd opened up last time. Once the insulation was done, he'd ask if he could paint his room. It was still in baby colors, pale yellow, pale green.

Dan started the insulation the next week. He was real good at things like that. Grandma said she'd believe it when she saw it, but Mama brought home some material from the store to make curtains with. "It's too thin, really," she said, "but it'll do 'til we get some better." Jesse was going to help over the weekend. Weekdays, it was nearly dark by the time he got back from school, and they hadn't had the electric turned on again. They didn't have the oil burner going either, and Dan said for his next job he was gonna insulate an igloo.

Thursday night it started to snow and Jesse thought for sure they'd have a snow day. First thing Friday morning he saw the light coming in his window was that flat bright everywhere-at-once light that you get when there's snow on the ground, and he put the radio on to hear the announcements even before he went to look out the window. The truck was gone and its tracks were in the new snow. He knew Dan was gone. He said out loud to himself, "I bet he's over to the house, startin' work early," but he knew he was gone.

Downstairs, Mama was at the table crying and Grandma was standing at the stove, but Jesse couldn't see that she was cooking. Mama's face looked as if she'd been crying for hours and hours. Puffed up like bug bites.

"Did you and him fight?" Jesse asked, wondering why he hadn't heard.

"I never got the chanst," she said. "He just took off. I would 'a fought. I would 'a said he cain't do us this way. I would 'a told him…" She put her head on her arms on the table and Jesse could barely hear her say, "I guess that's why he just took off. He never could stand bein' told."

Grandma came and sat down and beckoned to Jesse to sit on her lap. He was too big, really, his heels dragging the floor and his elbows sticking out, but she put her arms around him and he rested his head by her shoulder, where her collarbone would have been if you could feel it through her flesh. She sat and rocked him like a baby, and Mama sat with her head on her arms and nobody said anything.

It wasn't a snow day after all, and Jesse begged to be allowed to stay home. "I want to take care of Mama," he said.

"Well, there's no need, because you're goin' to school and I'm goin' to work."

"Honey," her mother said, "Do you really want to go with…feelin' the way you do?"

"It don't matter what I feel like! I cain't afford to lose a day's pay on top of ever'thing else. And I won't feel no different tomorrow."

"Honey…" but she didn't listen, just went and washed her face again.

In a way, it was better being at school. At school he was the only one that was sad, so he could forget about it once in a while.

His friend Daniel asked him if anything was the matter and he said that his dad had to go away.

"Well, don't feel bad about that," he said. "He's coming back, isn't he?"

"'Course."

"Shoot, my dad goes away all the time. There's not enough work around here to keep him busy, he says. He calls every night, though. Does your dad call?"

"Sure. Sure he does."

"Well, you don't need to feel bad. Just think how bad he's gonna feel when you grow up and leave home! Just think about that!"

Jesse did.

At lunchtime he went into the chapel. He was allowed. "The chapel is the heart of the school," Pastor Happold said. "You're always welcome there." Jesse had decided he would sit and think about his father, but really, once he had put himself into his usual seat, he didn't think of anything much. It got darker while he sat there and he wondered whether it was fixin' to snow again and if they'd send the bus children home early. He smelled the varnish and paint of the place and looked at the snowlight coming through the clear panes. He kind of wished there was an angel with a red robe in the window to color the light, like there was in Mount Calvary, but it didn't matter. If you kept looking you could see colors in the glass anyhow, the way the clouds moved over it and the reflections of the outdoors came and went.

Grandma came to pick him up after school and she asked him how he was.

"Okay." They drove on for a ways. "How's Mama?"

"I haven't been home yet."

"Was ever'body workin' today?"

"I guess."

"Where do you think my daddy is now?"

"I don't know…" Her voice ended on an upward note, as though the sentence had another half that she didn't say.

"D'you think he'll come back?"

"You're askin' the wrong person entirely, Jesse."

"I wish he would come back, Grandma."

"Precious, I know you do, but… well, sometimes it's hard for us to know what to wish for."

"I'll pray about it."

"Well, that's always a good thing, Jesse. If you take your burdens to the Lord, you'll see how they get lighter to bear."

Aunt Alice was there when he got home. She was standing at the table covering a big square cake with white icing. Mama sat with her hands on the table before her lying quiet on either side of a bowl. It made Jesse uncomfortable to see her sitting still. She never did, usually.

Grandma said, "Well, I brought him home. I guess we'll have to keep him, now."

Mama looked up and smiled at him. Her face wasn't as puffy as it was this morning, but there was still something wrong with it. Specially when she smiled.

Aunt Alice wiped her hands on the dishtowel she had over her shoulder and came to hug him. "Hey, honey," she said. "Are you feelin' okay?"

Jesse shrugged. "I guess," he said.

"Well, you will be, darlin'. You and me and Mama and your mama, we'll take care of each other, won't we?"

He shrugged again. He wanted to speak, to agree, but he couldn't.

"Well, you come over here and make me some pink icin' I need for the edge of this cake. It's for a 40th birthday. Why anybody should celebrate that, I do not know, but they asked for it, so…"

She interrupted herself to lean across the table and slide the glass bowl away from in front of Edith and put it at an empty place. "Now you put down that stuff and wash your hands," she said to Jesse. "And here's the cochineal. Whatever you do don't put too much in or I'll have to mix up more white."

Edith looked up. "Oh, Alice, I don't know what's the matter with me. I meant to do that. Give it here."

"Well, I know what's the matter with you. Never mind, Jesse'll do just fine, won't you, Jesse?" Jesse nodded. "I don't know why anybody has to do it; I should a' brought some ready mixed, but there you are. I didn't and it's poor little Jesse's got to pay the price."

"If that's the hardest work poor little Jesse ever has to do he'll be luckier than most," said Grandma.

"I don't care how hard I work," said Jesse.

"Bless your heart, I know you don't. I'm just jokin'," said his grandmother. "You sit down here and I'll put on a pot a' coffee. You want some hot milk and syrup, Jesse?"

"That's a baby drink," he said. "Can I have a coke?"

"As cold as it is? Well, if you can find a can in the ice box you can have it."

He hesitated. "I'll have a cup a' coffee," he said.

"Well, I never did." But when the coffee was made she poured him a cup. "Put in plenty of sugar, darlin' and it won't taste so bad."

†

"Mama," he said, "Do you think Dad's comin' back?" This was later, when she was back like herself.

"Jesse," she said, "I wouldn't have him back."

"Mama, you would, too."

"Jesse, he can't go on treatin' us this way. What are we supposed to be? We're not a vacation. Just for when he hasn't got anything else to do."

"But don't you love him anymore?"

She sighed, "I don't see as it makes much difference either way, Jesse."

"But he's my dad."

"He sure acts like it, too."

"Oh, Mama."

When he asked his grandma, she said, "You better talk to your mama."

"I did. She says she won't have him around no more."

"Well then."

"But she don't mean it."

"You reckon."

"Does she mean it?"

"I think she does, Jesse. At least she does now. Don't ask me what she'll say the next time he turns up."

"I guess we won't move back to the house now, though, will we, Grandma?"

†

People didn't get asked to lead prayer group. Usually one of the teachers did it, but if none of them was there, then anybody could start. Or sometimes even if one was. Whoever felt moved. Pastor Happold said not to worry if you never felt moved to preach. It was a gift of the spirit, like speaking in tongues and those gifts were not distributed equally. Everybody had different gifts. Just listening and being obedient was a gift, too. Girls couldn't be called to preach, for instance, but they could be just as good Christians as a man. This worried Jesse a bit. His grandma had a cousin—some kind of cousin—Sister Mary Mercy, and she preached all over. People would come from miles around to hear her. Grandma took him to listen to her once at homecoming at her church. This was when he was little, before he started at Christ the King, before he was even baptized, and he'd been baptized when he was ten. And she preached all day. And she healed and spoke in tongues. She was a big woman and she had lots of gray speckled hair tied up on the top of her head and she wore a long dark red dress and it was the most exciting preaching Jesse had ever heard. People were crying all day, they were so touched by the conviction of their sin, and there was speaking in tongues all over the room. And people falling down with the healing. Jesse wanted to cry himself, not because of his sinfulness but because...he didn't know why. He was just so...something. Something high, like a string inside him was being pulled upward and the whole day he breathed hard as though he'd been running. He didn't cry and he didn't come down to the Mercy Seat and give himself to Jesus, but he'd always thought the Holy Spirit was in that room, and that's what was doing all the pulling and making the people shout. But if Sister Mary Mercy wasn't really called to preach, then it must not have been the Holy Spirit after all. So what was it?

But anyhow, at Christ the King the women didn't preach. Or girls. They had women teachers, but that's because they were children. Women could be called to teach children, and other women, but not men. "What would we do without our women?" Principal Lowell said. He meant for teaching the children.

One of the boys—Jesse knew his name was Michael, but he didn't know him; he was in the secondary department—stood up and said, "Dear God our heavenly father, thank you for our teachers and our parents and for the chanst we have to become good Christian men and women and thank you for this good weather we've been havin' after our real cold winter and please God help us to honor your name and be faithful to your will and God...we know it ain't right to pray for anything that's bad for other people, but if it be thy precious will please let us win the basketball tonight in the name of the Lord Jesus Christ, Amen." Some people laughed and some said amen. Jesse said amen. He was going to the basketball game. He knew he wasn't ever going to be tall enough to play high school basketball, but he knew a lot about it, and he liked it. He was fast on the court, but besides not being tall enough, he wasn't very accurate. Just the same, he liked playing with the kids. There was talk that Michael was going to leave Christ the King next year and go to Catawba High so he could go play basketball there. One of the girls in Jesse's class said he was hoping to get an athletic scholarship to college, and Catawba had a lot better facilities. Most of the older boys left at that age.

When Jesse stood up, he wasn't even sure what he was going to say, only he felt moved at least to stand up.

"Dear Heavenly Father," he said, "We thank you for all our good homes and our good lives and we pray you make us remember all those children in the world who don't know your glorious name or your son's name that is Jesus Christ our Lord." A few people said amen and he went on, picking up speed. "Dear Heavenly Father, we pray you make us faithful unto death, because we know that the world is going to vanish away like smoke and the heavens are going to be rolled up like a scroll but thy heavenly kingdom will last forever and we won't last forever but we will be like grass before the mowers and the moth will eat us up like a garment and the moth will eat us like wool except if we're in your heavenly kingdom and we pray that you let us come into it. And we know that at the end of time the whole world will be like the best party in the world, with all the lost and strayed sheep found and carried home and the hearts of the fathers will be turned to the children and the hearts of the children will be turned to the fathers and peace will flow like a river and righteousness like a stream."

"Amen." Everyone was watching him now, but he was looking over their heads, through the clear pane of glass into the shifting light.

"And we shall be borne upon your sides and dandled on your knees and we will suck and be satisfied with the breasts of your consolation." No one spoke. "And we will milk out and be delighted with the abundance of your glory and we shall be comforted in Jerusalem and our bones will flourish like a herb. Amen." He looked at the others, who were looking at him. "We pray in the name of your blessed son our Lord Jesus Christ, Amen." The others said amen and Jesse sat down.

Pastor Happold spoke from the doorway. "Thank you, Jesse. I will just lead us now in a closing prayer that we may enter our afternoon's work refreshed to glorify Him in all that we do."

Jesse hadn't known Pastor Happold had been listening to him. He hadn't hardly been listening himself. God had been listening.

When Grandma got there to pick him up in the car, Pastor Happold walked out with him and leaned down to the window while Jesse walked round to the other side to get in.

Grandma started to open the door, but she couldn't because Pastor Happold was leaning into the window. Jesse knew it would make her uncomfortable to be sitting while the pastor had to bend over to talk to her.

"We were real proud of Jesse this dinnertime," he said.

"Is that right?" She looked around at Jesse, who was settling into the seat.

"I should say so," he said. "He gave us a real good sermon in prayer meeting."

"Did he?"

"He surely did." He paused for a moment, looking into Grandma's face. "Did you know that Jesse is American for Jesus?"

"Well, now…"

"Yes ma'am. If Jesus had 'a been born in America, the angels would have said to name him Jesse. That's the truth."

"Well, now…"

"Now, Jesse don't you be gettin' the wrong idea." He was smiling broadly.

"No, sir."

"Only…" Pastor Happold stuck his head a little further inside the car and lowered his voice. Jesse could still hear him. "Only there's some parts of the Bible—in particular in the Old Testament—that's a little bit strong for a boy. Do you know what I mean?"

"Well, I sure don't, Pastor."

"In particular in the Book of Isaiah."

Grandma shook her head.

"He can't go wrong with the gospels," said Pastor Happold. "Now, I'd never tell a boy not to read any part of the Good Book, only a boy needs…sometimes a boy needs a strong hand," he said.

Grandma nodded, frowning.

Pastor Happold pulled his head out and straightened up slowly, putting his hand to the small of his back. "Well," he said, "you have a safe journey home, now. Be good, Jesse. God bless you," and he waved as they drove away. "See you tomorrow morning!"

"I did good, Grandma, didn't I?"

"Well, I guess you did, Jesse."

"Grandma, did you know that my name was American for Jesus?"

"No, I surely did not know that."

"Grandma, did you know that once I heard a angel's voice?"

"Now, Jesse…"

"No, honest. I did. It was right after Daddy left that time. Do you remember that?"

"I do."

"Well, I saw such a beautiful face up in the air—only you could see through it, so I knew it wasn't earthly—and I heard a voice. Only it was a voice…it might ha' been in my head or it might ha' been out in the chapel, I couldn't tell, but I know I heard it."

"Well, Jesse, what did it say to you?"

"It said I was supposed to be some kind of a teacher or a preacher and bring people to the word of God."

"A teacher or a preacher?"

"I can't remember the exact words," he said. "I think it wasn't exactly in words. But it was real clear."

"Well, Jesse, I think that's a fine thing."

"Is it a callin' do you think?"

"It sure does sound like it."

"And just think of my name bein' the same as Jesus's name."

"Almost."

"Almost. Grandma."

"Jesse."

"Do you think it's better to be saved or be smart?"

"Now that's hard, Jesse. What do you think's better?"

"Well, I think it's better to be saved, because that lasts forever and ever. And I know I'm saved."

A Red Crayon

*Their children, which have not known any thing, may hear
and learn to fear the Lord.*
—Deuteronomy 31:13

Well, my brother-in-law was sayin' how you have to teach the young-uns to behave, and I think he's right. Well, I know he is, up to a point. You can't leave 'em to run wild. That's not doing them a favor.

But I know how he teaches his kids. Ooh, don't you think he tears them up! Now, I'm not one of these people who thinks you mustn't lay a hand on a child—your own child, I mean—I think I'd kill anybody else who hit a kid of mine. These people who say you mustn't spank a kid, well, mostly they don't have any kids of their own, do they? They're just some kind of college graduate. My grandmother used to say there's some things you can't learn out of books, and raisin' kids is surely one of 'em.

No, it's true, they have to learn. I don't hold with everything in the Bible, but "the rod and reproof give wisdom," is about right. You know, when it says "rod," it sounds bad, but I expect it only means a switch. But you know how it goes on about how a child left to himself brings shame to his mother, and I think that's true. Well, you can't expect a child to raise itself. But Martin—my brother-in-law Martin—he goes too far sometimes, I think. Well, to tell you the truth, I know for a fact he does. Of course I'd never say so. My sister is the one to say that to him, not me, but you know she never will. It's my opinion that she doesn't exactly agree with him, but—it's hard to know how to say this right—she's not so sure he's wrong that she feels right interfering. He is the head of the house. And you can't show them that Mom and Dad don't agree, can you? You have to have a united front. They'll just play one off against the other if you don't. But I've been there while my sister Annie was just cryin' her eyes out, listening to him givin' that little boy a whuppin'. She'd flinch ever'time she heard that belt hit just as

29

if it was landin' on her. But she never said a word to him when he came out. Just went and took care of Daniel. I wished I wasn't there, 'cause Martin and me was together in that front room. Not a sound, except for that child cryin'—he's only seven, no more than a baby—and him slidin' that ol' belt back through the loops of his pants, and I couldn't think of a word to say to him that wouldn't have been the start of a fight. I wouldn't 'a minded fightin' with him, but that would just about of tore Annie right up. She just hates it when folks fight. I don't mind it.

I'll tell you one thing, my mamma don't like the way he does. One time she said to my sister, "Annie, hasn't that husband of yours ever heard 'Vengeance is mine, sayeth the Lord'?" And I thought that was about right, since he's so big on the Bible. But you know, then I started to think that might be worse. The Lord's vengeance. You know, when you were little and you did some mischief, and your grandma or whoever was mindin' you might say, just you wait 'til your daddy gets home and I tell him what you've done. Well, don't it just spoil your whole day waiting? I think if you're waitin' for God to get home and whup you, it about spoils your whole life. Mind, I guess that's what the churches teach. So now you see. I'm not a real Christian. I believe in Jesus and the love of God, but I just haven't found a church that doesn't try to get people to behave by scarin' 'em to death. And that's the truth.

I'll just tell you a story. Years ago, when we lived in Bethesda Community—it was a real little place, then, just a few houses and the post office and some gas pumps and this little frame church; of course, now it's a lot bigger—got a supermarket and a garage and I don't know what all. But in those days my mama had to come right in to Drexel to go to work. She was a religious woman—she still is—and she used to haul us to church ever' Sunday, rain or shine, and we'd go to Sunday School and then we'd have to sit through the worship service with her and Daddy, my brother Sam and I did. I was young enough I didn't mind it so much. Sometimes I'd fall asleep on Daddy's lap, and I guess Mama thought some of that goodness would sink in anyway.

Well, Sam and I weren't in the same class, cause he was that little bit older. We didn't have Annie yet. She wasn't born 'til after we moved into town. The class I was in, it was just like kindergarten really, only we colored in scenes from the Bible instead of—oh, you know, firemen and ducks on ponds. Ballet dancers. Well, this one day the teacher gave out these pictures. Now, looking back on it, I suppose they were pretty much like all the other pictures, but they were meant to be stained glass windows. With those pointed tops, you know? And lines through 'em, so it looked like the lead between the pieces of colored glass. I expect there was a Bible verse, but I don't remember. I just thought they were just the most beautiful pictures. I wasn't but tee-tiny. Mine was of the dove coming down to Jesus when he was standin' in the river to be baptized so I had all that blue water and green trees I could do. I knew to leave Jesus's robe the color of the paper, but I decided to make John the Baptist's robe red, and I picked up this crayon and it came out just the most beautiful color. Just like wine—not that you'd think of that in a Baptist church, would you?—just like grape juice. I was wearin' a little summer dress that my mom made me, with puffed pockets sewn on the front both sides, and I just dropped that crayon in my pocket. I never did work out why I did that; it just seemed to find its own way in there. It seems like it was the color I wanted to keep. But once I put it in, it never seemed the right time to take it out.

Well, after a while it got time to sit on the rug for our Bible story, and I can't even remember what the story was, but I do remember that the teacher told us about the Ten Commandments, so maybe it was the golden calf one. Then she told us about hell—the ever-burning fire, and the dark smoke smelling of sulphur. Oh, I tell you, she was a one for paintin' a picture. She spoke so clear I tell you I could just feel the heat comin' off that lake of burnin' brimstone. And it wasn't only me, either. Even the big boys—well, I say big, of course all of us wasn't nothin' but babies, but they seemed big to me; you know how much there is between four and four and a half when you're that age—even the big boys was listenin' with big eyes, and there was just one big shudder through us all when she said how we'd hear the big iron door to heaven bang shut over our heads never to be opened again forever and ever. Oh, she could tell a tale, all right.

So then she got back to the Ten Commandments. Or that's how I remember it. Now, she might have talked about all of 'em, but I don't suppose she did. We were too little to know what most of 'em meant, after all. But she talked about honoring my father and my mother—I just made up my mind not to sass back—and then about lyin' (I guess it must a' been false witness, now that I think about it), and I thought, well, I won't ever do that. But stealing. She said, "Now children, you must promise me and promise the Lord Jesus that you will never steal, because that's about the lowest thing a person could do." And everybody said, "I promise!" except for me. And I couldn't say it. It was like that red crayon was stuck in my throat like to choke me if I tried. And I felt as if ever'body could hear me bein' quiet. Really, I don't suppose anybody noticed. I mean, now I think about it all these years gone by, a roomful of toddlers—we were hardly any more than that—would shout out just about anything you tell 'em, just to join in with the noise, and if there's one who doesn't—well, it doesn't mean anything. She could just have lost interest. Oh, but I hadn't lost interest. I was plotting how I could get that red crayon back in its box and save my poor soul. The trouble was that the play equipment was all put away by then, in cupboards. I didn't even know which cupboard the crayons went in, but I had a awful feelin' it was gonna be one that was too high for me to reach. I could have left it just layin' on the table, but you know, I couldn't make up my mind to do that. I remember it just as clear. It seemed like I wouldn't have undone the stealing unless I got it right back where it was supposed to be. You know these ideas that children get... I went and pulled a chair over to one of them big cabinets and started to climb up on it—I guess I thought I was gonna try 'em all—and of course Miss Harben came over and lifted me down and said, now Peggy Mae, what are you tryin' to do? And she laughed and put me on my feet and put the chair back under the table. The parents had started to come in to pick up their children and she shook her head and said, you never know what they'll do next, do you? So everybody shook their heads and said you sure don't, and my mama and daddy were there for me and that was the end of it. I went off out of that little church with that crayon in my pocket and I want to tell you I never carried anything so heavy in my life, before or since. All the way back to the car, my brother was caperin' down the road and tryin' to get me to race him—cause he would always win, but I used to run against him ever'time. I think I thought I'd catch up with him one day and not be the youngest any more. But not this time. This day I wouldn't do a thing. Just plodded along 'til I got lifted into our big ol' Dodge and set off to home. And I heard my mama say, she's tired, and I felt like the biggest sinner in the world. Here she was feelin' sorry for me and I didn't deserve it a bit.

But I guess she must a' been right about me bein' tired, because I know for a fact that I slept all night that night, even though I was afraid to say my prayers. No, it was the next night I woke up with a nightmare. You know, to this day I can't remember what it was, but Mama told me I was screamin' like a crazy thing, and when she came into our room, I kept lookin' over her shoulder with my eyes so wide and scared that she couldn't help lookin' behind her, scared she'd see what I saw, even though she knew better.

Well, it took a week of nightmares before she got it out of me. Every night I was awake—or halfway awake and halfway still in my bad dream—and she told me—oh, this would a' been years later— that she thought there was getting to be something wrong with my mind. I never remembered the dreams, or even if they were different or always the same one, but I know I always woke up with the same bad feeling. Sick and scared.

I carried that crayon with me everywhere. I took it out of my dress pocket and put it in my sweater, and at night I'd put it under my pillow if my pj's didn't have a pocket. I don't know what I was thinkin', but I know I thought I had to have it by me. I must have left red smears on everything I wore, but Mama either didn't notice or she didn't think it was any one thing. Kids make enough mess, don't they?

One mornin' I couldn't find my pajamas when I went to get it out of the pocket, and I like to go crazy lookin' for it. Well, all that happened, of course, is my mama had put the washin' in first thing, and it went in with the dirty clothes. I've thought about this a lot, and I think I must ha' been ready to get caught, you know? Found out? Because I remember in the first days having that crayon in my fist while I was changin' clothes. I wouldn't leave it for a minute. I was gettin' careless, I guess. I can laugh about it now. It must a' been makin' me tired out, though. Really.

When she found it, when she was hangin' out the clothes, it was kind of deformed and squashed up, and she came in and asked me what it was. Well, of course that was it. I just sat down and howled. I'd tried to keep her from findin' out how bad I was and now she knew, and I know I was so sorry to let on but you know I must a' been kind of relieved at the same time. She just sat and listened to me. I think now it must have been a job to know what I was talkin' about, but she just let me keep on until she got it. She hugged me and kissed me and told me I was the best little girl in the world and not a sinner. And the next Sunday she took me to church and let me hand that damned crayon back. It must have been funny, you know, for everybody but me. Here was this poor old beat up crayon bein' handed over as if it was some kind of a prize, and me just in a tremble over it, and I expect Miss Harben didn't have the notion of an idea what was goin' on. At first. Mother said that I carried the crayon home "by mistake" is what she said, and she said that I had been afraid all week that I was going to hell. "Oh, my," Miss Harben said, and she bent over to me. "Why, Jesus who loves all the little children wouldn't let that happen, would he?" And then she kind of laughed and straightened up and said to my mother, "But it's good to know she's learned right from wrong so young, isn't it?"

Then Miss Harben put the crayon in the box and gave me a little pat on my head, and said that we were fixin' to have a real good time that mornin' and my mother took me by the hand and said, "She will never come to this place again, nor me nor anybody who belongs to me. No place that frightens children is a place of religion." And out we walked.

We joined a Church of Christ after that. Mother couldn't have lived without some kind of religion. But once I grew up, I found out I could. Not without religion, maybe, but church. It seems to me they all preach the same thing: "The fear of God is the beginning of wisdom."

Like my sister's little boy fears his daddy.

The Mountains of Spices

*Intreat me not to leave thee, or to return from
following after thee.*

—Ruth 1:16

Ruth knew that she had an important name. Almost as early in her
life as she had learned to point to herself and say "Ruth!"—or, in
those days, Rut'—she knew that her name was in the Bible. Ruth
had a book to herself in the Old Testament and she was the grandmother of David, who played on a harp and killed a giant when
he was still a little boy and grew up to be king, and she was the
great-great-many greats-grandmother of Jesus. She knew that Ruth
had declared, "Whither thou goest I will go. Thy people shall be
my people and thy god my god," but not until they got to Ruth in
Sunday School did she find out that she had not said those words
to her husband.

"She said that to her daddy's mommy!" she protested to her
mother when they met after the service. She was only five and
though she was quite clear on relationships, she did not always have
the vocabulary for them.

"Her husband's mommy," her mother corrected. "Her mother-
in-law. Naomi."

Ruth nodded. "I know!" she insisted. Then, "Who is a
mother-in-law?"

"Your husband's mom is your mother-in-law. Your baby's
grandma."

"Like Grandma Rose?"

Penny smiled. "Grandma Rose is *my* mommy, so she's Daddy's
mother-in-law. Grandma Daisy is my mother-in-law."

Ruth absorbed this genealogical information without too much
difficulty. Grown-ups talked a lot about how people were related,
and her two flowery grandmothers often argued, out of vast and
ancient knowledge, the minutiae of family connections.

"So why did she?"

"Why did she what, Sweetness?" Penny was always glad to encourage her youngest child's interest in the Bible, but she was distracted now, with the crowded afternoon to come.

"Why did she say whither thou goest and all to her mother-in-law?" Ruth tried to imagine her mother's saying such a thing to Grandma Daisy.

"Well. Because she loved her so much, I suppose. And respected her." Ruth knew about respect. She had a long list of people she was expected to respect. In 1986, Penny was doing her best to reproduce for her own children the values of her own upbringing, thirty years before. "After all," Penny went on, "if somebody raises up a man good enough to marry you, she must be pretty good, too."

Ruth thought. "That man was dead that she married."

"Yes, that's sad, isn't it?"

"And you know what?" said Ruth. "His name was Ophir."

"Was it, Sugar?"

Ruth nodded. "That's a funny name," she said. "Mommy..."

Penny was looking back a little irritably toward the church. She had expected Sam and the boys to have caught up with them by now. But no, Sam was standing around talking and Amos and Duncan were tearing through the shrubbery dirtying their clean clothes while Paul, who was old enough to be responsible, was shouting, egging them on.

"Mommy..."

"Yes, Sugar."

"Do you have to respect your husband's mommy?"

"Of course. She should be almost like your own mother to you."

Ruth thought. "But you still have your own mommy."

"Of course you do," and she smiled at her very young, so adorable child. Her only girl.

"Mommy, didn't Ruth have a mother?"

"Well, she might have had one someplace." Penny knelt and gave Ruth a hug, as though to reassure her that her own mother was present and would be able to look after her for years and years.

"But she loved Naomi so much."

"Well now, she surely did."

†

Most of Ruth's cousins, like her brothers, started life with hair of that almost white blondness that was locally called tow-headed. Her cousins started out fair and darkened to brown as they grew up. Ruth only darkened from tow to gold. The down on her arms and the back of her neck was gold. Only her eyebrows and lashes changed to a true brown. She had high breasts and a round bottom and long thighs made muscular by summers spent playing outdoors. She was a good soccer player and a strong long distance runner. She was the object of adolescent lust, and probably of more mature longings, but she was treated with respect. Her mother always said that if you act like a lady you'll be treated like one. Besides, she was a girl with three brothers. Despite her beauty, she wasn't the most pursued girl in school. Boys out for mere fun and a feel looked elsewhere, among the less protected.

When she was sixteen, she brought home her first boyfriend. Sam and Penny had discussed when to let her date, but their decision did not, in the end, matter very much. Sam was inclined to be indulgent, and even Penny had finally to accept that Ruth could not be controlled as she had been controlled. Luckily, Will could be accommodated. A few months older and a few inches taller than Ruth, he was an okay student, not impressively bright but not too dumb. Though not husband material, he was an acceptable boyfriend: athletic, polite, a churchgoer. He already knew Ruth's brothers; he played basketball with Duncan.

But whenever she went out, Penny looked after her anxiously. That child, she thought, has no idea how beautiful she is, has no idea how dangerous this world is. Once she said to Sam, "It just hurts my heart to let her go," and he laughed and said, "She's tougher than you think."

She didn't go out with Will for very long. She liked him all right. He was super good looking, and a good kisser. But she never missed him when he wasn't there.

She spent the summer she turned seventeen without a boyfriend, untroubled. She cycled with her friends and they went for picnics and swam in the cold water up in the mountains, where you could get bit by a water moccasin if you didn't look out, and in the pool at the Athletic Center. She and her girlfriends dressed up and went out dancing in the town's one, rather tame club or at the youth center. She didn't drink because it made her sick. She went fishing with her brother Amos. She would be a junior in the coming fall. Two more years of high school and then... the rest of her life.

In the fall she met Roger, and dated him the whole of her junior year. He was a football player and already had an athletic scholarship to State. He was tall, blond like her, blue-eyed like her, and he came from nice people. Whenever they got the chance, they necked passionately in the back of his father's vintage Chevy, which had plenty of room. They were hungry and thirsty for each other, hurried and hot, but they stopped, each time, before Roger had the occasion to use one of his carried hopefully condoms. Roger was importunate, but respectful, and Ruth was firm. She didn't exactly think that God was watching her at every moment (even when she went to the toilet) as she had when she was small, but she believed there was such a thing as sin, and that having sex with Roger would unarguably be sin. She had a feeling that her baptism and her church membership and her status as Sunday school teacher, all amounted to a promise to be good. And she was determined not to give her virginity up in the back seat of a car—even a vintage Chevy—with somebody she knew, however good he felt, she wouldn't love for long. And besides, her mother would have a fit.

Roger went away to university and they both promised to write, and they did, but when he came home for Thanksgiving they didn't quite pick up where they had left off. They never exactly broke up, but during the Christmas vacation they didn't see much of each other. Their families sent cards.

By then, only one of Ruth's three brothers was living at home, and he was engaged to be married, so Ruth found a boyfriend who was like a brother: funny and smart and easy to be with. Her parents included him in family occasions and felt lucky that their daughter was so sensible.

Then she met Wesley late in the spring of her last year of high school. They had been in the same school all along, only she hadn't noticed him before. Hadn't really seen him. If she had gone on not seeing him for just another month, her life would not have taken the turn it did. She would not have lost her parents, to whom she had been an answered prayer, and her brothers, who had spent most of their youths protecting her. Even three more weeks.

Nobody was going out much, in spite of the beautiful weather, because it was exams, and parents were anxious. Ruth stayed in on Friday evening and on Saturday they all went out to eat with her brother Paul and his fiancée. It had been Ruth's job to find out what Jasmine wanted for her wedding shower without asking her. It was supposed to be a surprise, but of course it wouldn't be. "If she doesn't have a shower, she'll be the first girl in this county not to since the War Between the States," Ruth said to her mother. It turned out that she wanted towels. Poor Paul, Ruth thought. Towels.

She settled down to her history notes as soon as she got home. She had always been a reasonably diligent student, but she wasn't a star. Now there was nothing she could do but work hard. She wasn't exactly worried, but she wasn't exactly confident. "Don't stay up too late," Penny said when she went to bed. "You'll learn more when you're rested."

When she came to wake her daughter up the next morning, Penny found Ruth at her desk. "Mercy, Ruth, you haven't been sitting there all night!"

"No, of course I haven't. I got up early and I thought I'd do some work before church—and I hope I don't die today." Grandma Rose always said "Well, I hope he don't die today," when she saw someone working on the Sabbath and it had entered family folklore. Ruth always thought it sounded more like a curse than a prayer. Familiar though it was, it made Penny smile.

"Well, I'm just putting the coffee on. Come down when you hear it perkin'." She paused at the doorway. "You dressed for church?"

Ruth looked down at the jeans and t-shirt she was wearing as though she had not seen them for a longish time. "No," she said. "I just put any old thing on. I'll get changed."

Her mother brought her a cup of coffee and pulled out the little leaf in her desk to place it on. "I'm not bringing eggs up here," she said. "You'll have to come down if you want breakfast."

Ruth shook her head. "No, that's okay. I don't really want anything. This is nice, though," and she reached for the cup.

"Well, I'm going to get ready. You keep watching the clock now."

When Penny came back, she allowed herself an exasperated sigh. "Honey, you're gonna have to hurry."

"Mom," she turned around and looked up. "You know, I think I won't go. I'm not teachin' the little ones this morning; the congregation can spare me for one Sunday."

"Well, maybe they can, Ruth, but..."

"Mom, I know God understands about this exam; it's taken me a million years to finally get goin' on it and if I stop now I'll never get started again. If He hadn't let all this history happen, I wouldn't be havin' such a hard time."

"You ever heard of blasphemy?"

Ruth laughed. "It's just a little joke."

"Well, it's up to you. We'll miss you."

"I'll see you later, Mom. I could be finished with this part by the time you get back. Only tell Grandma I've got a headache or something. God can take a joke, but I don't think Grandma Daisy can."

"Don't push your luck, Miss." But she was smiling.

A few minutes later, when the door closed behind Ruth's mother, father, and brother, she was back at work. She was wasting time over the XYZ Affair, in a way. They'd never want her to know as much as she was learning. But it was interesting. The textbook said there had been an undeclared war. She wondered how you knew when it was finished, if it was undeclared. And how did you even notice it had started? Well, she thought, at least nobody got shot. And you could always find a way to work extra knowledge into an answer; there was a chance it would impress, even if it was irrelevant.

She moved her over-elaborate notes on the Adams administration to the back of her folder, got herself back on track and worked through to the end of her outline. Then she stood up and stretched. It was nearly one o'clock and she had hardly moved from her desk since she sat down at six that morning. She was proud of herself for her concentration, the intensity of her attention. She felt like a real student.

"I'll have a walk," she said out loud, and, full of her accomplishment, she added, "for the time of the singing of birds is come."

The pavement under her feet glittered a little with the mica in the concrete. Once Elder Springs had only had hard dirt sidewalks that must have gone to slush in wet weather. "Constructed WPA" was stamped on some of the pavement squares. All those men, she thought, out of work and no social security in those days. Her grandparents remembered the Great Depression. She had interviewed them a couple of years ago for a project. Grandma Daisy said that they were pretty lucky in North Carolina. "Things weren't so bad here." But Granddad was from Tennessee. "There were children on the roads," he had said, shaking his head. "I hope to the Lord you never see anything like it. Children walkin' the roads huntin' work or food or just a place to lay down." Their families couldn't feed them. Their fathers couldn't provide. Granddad traveled in those days. He was a skilled man and he got by. "I got by," he said, "on account of I had just myself. I would a' hated to a' been a family man in those days." He must have been a boy, really, she thought, a skilled boy. But the Works Progress Administration had paid men to build the sidewalks, which glittered now with mica under her white sneakers. Ruth thought how joyfully they must have poured the concrete, knowing that they would get money for groceries at the end of the week. That was Roosevelt (1932-1945), and it was why Granddad was a Democrat till the day he died. Mr. Oaks, who lived on Catawba Avenue, remembered when even the big road coming into town was laid with half logs that sank into the mud in the early spring rains. He and his father used to haul wood to lay over them. The wood had to be pulled by mules. Mr. Oaks must be pretty old, she thought, older than her grandparents, but even so, that was recent to have had mud roads. He had once pointed to the smart houses across from his place. "In them days," he said, "there warn't nothin' over there but nigger shacks. Yessir, just nothin' but tarpaper shacks." And he shook his head at the progress he had seen.

She walked briskly, as though she had a destination, but really she was going where her feet led her. She passed the black church just as it was letting out. They had longer services, she knew, than most white churches did. And livelier ones. She had visited a black church—not this one—with her friend Annie from school a couple of times. Her family was Holiness. Ruth liked the preaching and the singing there. She told Annie who said, "Don't get too carried away with all that black soul. You try one of the AME churches one time; they're as dull as if they were white." She smiled now, remembering it, pleased to think that Annie could tease her so comfortably, as though being black or white were no more than a dress you put on. Still smiling, she paused to let a woman dressed in a butter-yellow coat hurry three little boys in powder blue suits from the church steps to a car waiting at the curb. Still smiling, she looked up and saw Wesley standing between a man and a woman she supposed were his parents. They were talking across him, arguing amiably. He was looking into Ruth's face.

When her way was clearer, she moved through the family groups and the circling children. Her path took her to Wesley. "Hey," he said, when she was within speaking distance. The woman had taken a few steps away and she looked back as he spoke. "Mama," he said, "this is Ruth McBride. She's a friend from school." Ruth turned toward Wesley's mother. She was a tall, very dark woman wearing a navy blue dress and a white hat trimmed in blue. "Ruth," Wesley went on, "I'd like you to meet my mother and..." he gestured to the round-faced man who was walking back toward them, "my dad."

"How do you do," she said, feeling constrained to an unfamiliar formality by Wesley's demonstration of good manners.

"Well, hello Ruth," said Wesley's mother. She extended her hand and grasped Ruth's, "It's a pleasure. My name's Margaret."

"Oh, that's my middle name. Or nearly. It's Marguerite—it's like a daisy. It's kind of after my grandma Daisy."

"Well, that's a pretty idea, Ruth. But Margaret means pearl, too, you know. The kingdom of God is the pearl of great price."

The man laughed as he reached for her hand. "Well, this is a very godly conversation to be havin' on a Sunday morning I'd say. I'm James Middlewright."

She took his hand and smiled, grateful. She knew that Wesley was Wesley, but she had been trying to remember what his last name was. Middlewright. How could she have forgotten a name like that? Besides, they always used to be named together at roll call. Alphabetically united.

"Now, Ruth, are you goin' somewhere in particular?" asked Mrs. Middlewright.

It struck her that she was the worst-dressed person on the Sunday street. It seemed to require some explanation. "Not really," she said. "I've been studyin' all morning and I just came out for a walk to... sort of clear my head out."

The older woman nodded. "We're walkin' this way home," she said, nodding toward the direction from which Ruth had come. "If your walk takes you our way, perhaps you'd like to stop for a glass of tea as you pass."

Ruth hesitated for a moment, reflecting that she didn't even know Wesley. He had called her his friend, but that was just politeness, really. She had needed reminding of his last name. But she had turned as they talked and they were all facing the same way. It was only a glass of tea and a walk on a spring day. "All right," she said. "Yes, I will, thank you."

Wesley and his father had begun to walk along together and she and Mrs. Middlewright followed them. She walked pretty fast, Ruth thought. "Now," she said, "what is it you're studying?"

"Oh." She was a little surprised. It was the season of exams; everybody was studying one thing after another. What they were studying was exams. "Well, this morning I was studying history."

"Do you like history?"

"Yes," she answered, "I guess I do, really."

Mrs. Middlewright nodded. "You won't be able to get into it until after the exam," she said.

Ruth laughed. "That's right. I never thought about that. You haven't got time to get interested in anything. Not really interested."

The woman agreed, "I found it so, even at the University."

"You went to college?" She realized how rude her surprise must sound. Would apologizing make it worse?

"I surely did," Mrs. Middlewright said, with no sign that she was offended. "For a little while. It was going to take a long time to finish. I went to study law."

"I see." There were black lawyers and women lawyers on television, but she didn't think she'd ever met one of either, much less the two together. "You had to give it up?" It must be all right to ask. She wouldn't have mentioned it if she'd flunked out.

"Well, it got to be hard." Money, probably, Ruth thought. "Life takes its own path sometimes. I trained as a legal secretary instead. That's been interesting over the years."

By the time they got to the Middlewrights' ochre-yellow house, Ruth was ready to forget she was a stranger. They didn't go in. Ruth and the men sat on the front porch, Ruth on the long swing. James Middlewright asked questions, told little stories, laughed at everything she said. He was paler than his wife and had green-gray eyes, lighter than his skin. Wesley took after him more than his mother, Ruth decided, although Wesley was tall, like her. Mrs. Middlewright brought a pitcher of tea, misted with cold, and tall glasses on a tray. Ruth accepted hers gladly, but she did not linger. She could smell their Sunday dinner. The smell drifted out the front door, mixing with the cut-grass scent from next door where a Sabbath-breaking neighbor was mowing his lawn. She mustn't keep them. Besides, her own dinner would be waiting. She and Wesley had hardly exchanged a word. She looked over at him as she prepared to rise and say goodbye, and she found that he was looking into her face. That was the second time that had happened.

She told her mother and father and brother over dinner about her walk, about meeting the Middlewrights, about stopping for tea. She mentioned where it was they lived; she even repeated one of Wesley's father's jokes. There was nothing she did not tell them, and yet she felt there was something undisclosed.

Perhaps that was why she went on talking about him. He was in her history class. She wondered aloud whether they were in the same exam set. They had English together, too. He hadn't liked *Catcher in the Rye*. She had forgotten that, but now it came back to her. It must be hard to write an essay on a book you didn't like, didn't they think? She had liked *Catcher in the Rye*, but Wesley said that Holden Caulfield sounded like a spoiled rich kid to him and he couldn't get interested. Besides, Wesley said why weren't they reading something contemporary, something relevant?

"It sounds like your friend Wesley holds strong opinions," said Sam.

"Oh. I guess. I don't know really. I never paid much attention. It was just meeting him this morning. And exams coming up. That reminded me."

She glanced across the table at her brother. There was something unexpected in his face. She couldn't read it.

"What?" she asked him.

He shrugged and did not answer.

There was no reason for it, but she decided not to say anything more that brought Wesley's name into her mouth. Only then she couldn't think of anything to say. She waited for someone else to speak instead.

†

Later, she was to say that she had fallen in love with Wesley that day, that moment when she met his eyes across the bright pavement outside his church, but that she hadn't known it for another ten days. Wesley had known it all along.

They exchanged smiles and brief greetings in the corridors as they walked to and from exams. There was no occasion to touch. Nothing of significance was said. But always she felt the force of his dark gold eyes. Looking at him now, it astonished her that she had not noticed before how beautiful he was. She was drawn into the space around him; when they passed one another, it was an effort to maintain her direction, as though there were something in her body that wished not to walk away from him but to fall into an orbit of which he was the center. She was conscious of him all week and at the weekend she was conscious of his absence. On Wednesday, they kissed each other. They were walking side by side between buildings. Exams were over; everyone felt untethered at last. He said something—about a test question, about his plans for the summer, some little thing—and she turned her face to his, to answer, and their lips came together. Instantly she was drowned with love. They came apart, still looking into each other's eyes, laughing, relieved and frightened.

They were young, they said to each other, and they had their educations to get. They would wait, but one day they would marry. They would not wait to tell their parents; they would tell them right away. They wouldn't understand at first. They would probably oppose them. There would be problems, but they were young and smart and brave. And love is as strong as death.

Ruth was worried, but she was excited. She would say everything at once: Wesley and love and—not right away, but when they could—marriage. They would be surprised she had chosen someone black, even shocked. They would probably try to talk her out of it, but finally they would understand that it was no use, that she would not be moved. She would explain that she and Wesley were prepared for bigotry and abuse from ignorant people, that they could withstand it. That it would only make them stronger. In the end, they would accept it. And once they met Wesley, they would see. Finally they would be glad, happy because she was happy.

Mother cried. She had tears all over her face. She said, "Oh my God, have you...? Please tell me you haven't had sex with him."

"Well of course we haven't. What do you think I...?" Slightly guilty. Her mother didn't know how close she had come with Roger. She was glad now that she hadn't. Those True Love Waits people were fanatics, but there was something in what they said. She would be feeling terrible now if Wesley were not to be the first.

Her mother telephoned her father at work and told him, her voice choked and urgent, that he had to come home right away. He didn't even ask why; he was on his way. "It's not an emergency," Ruth said. "You're acting as if I was in the hospital or something!"

"I wish you were," said Penny.

It went on for days. Amos came home to join in.

Ruth said, "But, Daddy, you'll like him when you meet him. He comes from a nice family. He's a Christian."

"I don't care if he's Jesus Christ himself," said her father, "he's not screwing my daughter."

No one spoke; what he had said was so shocking, in so many ways.

Finally, into the electric silence, Grandma Rose said, "Now there's no need for language like that."

It was as though someone were dying. It was as though a storm had taken the roof off, as though they were refugees from a war, from a flood.

"We love each other," Ruth said.

"Love!" said her mother. Her voice was contemptuous, as though love were not worth mentioning.

Amos and Paul sat together in Paul's room with the door shut, talking. On the first day, Sam didn't go to work. Penny telephoned and told them he was sick. Ruth couldn't remember when her father had taken a sick day, not even when he really was sick.

"You're just going to have to give him up, Darling," said her mother.

"I won't," she said. "I can't."

"What if...just imagine he found another girl. Or died," she added quickly, before Ruth could speak. "You'd have to live without him, then. You'd have to get over it. Life would just go on, wouldn't it? Well..."

She paused, but Ruth did not speak.

"Well, it's just the same. You can just put him out of your mind. Oh, honey"—she reached out and put an arm around Ruth's rigid shoulders—"I know it won't be easy, but just think of him as...gone. Just grit your teeth and be strong. Just think of all those women who lost their fiancés in the war. In all the wars. Think how brave they had to be."

"I will be brave," said Ruth.

"Oh, I just know you will!"

"Not like you mean. I mean I'll stick by him forever. Whatever you do to me."

"Give him up," went on endlessly, from all of them. And then Sam said, "Don't get engaged right away. Wait a while. You're so young. You're both so young."

They were beginning to give way. "That's all right," she said. "We didn't expect to have a ring. Or an announcement in the paper. Only we'll still know we're engaged. We wouldn't want to keep it a secret."

"No, let's say you don't have anything to do with each other until you finish college."

She thought that she could not have understood. "Don't have anything...what do you mean? Not see each other?"

"And not write. Just until you finish college. If your feelings are as strong as you say, you can easy wait four years. If it doesn't last, then it just wasn't meant to be."

So there was no hope after all.

Sam overheard two of the men talking at work. At first he thought they had somehow found out about his Ruth, but it was just something in the paper. Some white actress was marrying a black man. The kind of thing they don't mind in Hollywood. The newspaper was lying between the men while they ate their sandwiches, a photograph uppermost. He nodded to them and walked by. They nodded back. "How can a woman like that...?" one of them asked. "Oh," said the other, "some women can't get enough of that ol' brown peter." They laughed. The first one sobered first. "If a daughter of mine was to take up with a jigaboo, I'd have to kill her," he said. But his friend disagreed. "Oh no," he said. "I could never harm a child of my own." He paused as long as a breath would take. "But I'd sure as hell have me one dead nigger!" and the two laughed together again.

Sam couldn't forget it. Than evening he said to Ruth, "You know I'd never let anybody harm a hair on your precious head."

"I know."

"But if I ever catch that nigger of yours, I swear I'll kill him."

Ruth could have cried real tears for her father. The threat was nothing. She knew he wouldn't murder anybody. It was the words. She felt bad for him, having said those things, and bad for herself, hearing them. Nothing like that had ever passed between them before.

They refused to meet Wesley, but he came to the door anyway, and Penny stood inside the screen door and spoke to him. Duncan, who had come home the night before, stood behind her with his arms folded across his chest, watching. Wesley stood firm on both feet, not shifting or fidgeting, but his face was anxious. Ruth hesitated on the upstairs landing, afraid she would make things worse if she tried to help.

"Ma'am," Wesley said. This was old fashioned of him. She had never heard him call anyone that before. "I just want you to know I love Ruth and I'll be good to her."

Penny said, "I'm sure you mean well. But it isn't up to you to be good to my daughter or otherwise. She has a family to do that."

"I just wanted to introduce myself to you," Wesley said.

"Well, you've done that now. I'll say goodbye," and she turned away from the door.

Duncan stepped forward and put his arm around his mother's shoulders. Wesley, on the other side of the screen door, stood looking at their united backs for a moment and then turned and went down the front steps. Ruth had started down the stairs, but Duncan and Penny were in the way and she could not have attracted his attention without shouting.

Even if they had wanted to, they couldn't watch her all the time. For one thing, Ruth had a job that summer; it had been arranged for months. She was to help out at the office of a friend of her uncle, moving jobs to cover regular staff as they took their vacations.

She started by helping Myrna in reception, filing and answering the phone. On the first day they invited her to have lunch with them but she said no and went to Wesley's house instead. She stood at the door long after she was sure no one was home. She leaned her head against the glass storm door, cooling her forehead. She had been running, and it was very warm. Then she fished around in the front pocket of her rucksack for her little spiral notebook. "Dear Wesley," she wrote. "I came to see you, but you were out." There seemed to be nothing else to write. Why write even that? At last she added, "I'm working at Wilkins Electrics, next to the Post Office." and then she signed her name. She longed to put "love" as she would on a note to the merest acquaintance, but she did not dare. She wrote just "Ruth" and left it in the letter slot. She had to hurry to get back by the end of lunch hour.

When he came to see her at work—not that day, but the next— she had been thinking about his lips. Lips were one of the features that got exaggerated in the ugly drawings you sometimes saw on leaflets from the white supremacists. "Just ignore it," her mother used to say, "those people are ignorant and full of hate." Fat lips. Wesley's were swollen like leaf buds, the color of a rose in his dark face, edged as sharply as though sculpted with a tool.

Myrna, who was showing her the ropes, was sitting at the counter saying how she'd thought they'd never have to hire another file clerk again once they got rid of the old typewriters ("Finally! We must a' been the last outfit in town to have those things!") but how they seemed to have more paper now than they ever did. "And you know some of that stuff never gets read again. Some of that stuff you're puttin' away right now won't ever get read again. I tell 'em but they don't listen. I thought we'd have got rid of those big old filin' cabinets by now but no, we have more paper now than we ever did have." It was Ruth's second day and she had heard this before; that was why she was able to think so intently about Wesley's mouth.

Myrna said, in a changed voice, "Hey there, how can I help you?" and Ruth turned, knowing that she would see Wesley standing in the doorway.

"Could I speak to Ruth, please?" he said, looking at Myrna and not at Ruth. "Just for a minute."

"I guess you don't want any electrical supplies," she said.

"No ma'am."

Myrna looked at Ruth and then at her watch. "Well, I guess we can afford that," she said. "A minute."

Ruth wondered if Myrna knew. If she did, it was kind of her, and dangerous, to give them their minute.

"I got your note," he said. It seemed a revealing remark. Myrna was looking at a sheaf of orders, but Ruth was pretty sure her attention was not on the papers.

She nodded, speechless with longing. The counter was between them.

"How are your parents?" he asked.

She shook her head. "They're pretty mad."

"Mine too," he said.

"Really?" That surprised her. She had been wrong, then, to expect them to be her allies. She had thought all the anger would come from her side. The white side. To think that they were not glad to get her...

He was smiling.

"I'll come over, shall I?" she said.

"Not right away." They were constrained, knowing they were overheard. "You quit at five?"

"Five fifteen."

"I'll see you then."

"Well. Okay."

He said, "Bye, now," and turned away.

"Friend of yours?" Myrna asked.

"Oh." She shrugged. "Just somebody I know from school. Sort of." She was ashamed of the "sort of." She was ashamed of the "just."

He met her as she walked home. She had been first disappointed, then bereft, when he hadn't been waiting for her. He joined her as she was crossing Appleyard Street. He had been waiting there. He was more wily than she.

This became the pattern of their meetings. They talked as they went along, laughing, lifted over their fear. But they did not touch, or only fleeting fingertips as they parted and he took the turning toward his parents' house. They did not kiss goodbye. Once Ruth saw her brother Duncan across the street. He was not looking at them and he went into the motorcycle showroom as they approached, but she knew he had seen them.

Margaret and James came home one lunchtime especially to meet with Ruth again. Wesley was not there. They did not seem angry. They were kind and wouldn't let her call them Mr. and Mrs. But James asked her if she had thought what a relationship with "a boy like ours" would mean, and when she said that yes, she had and that she could face anything, give up everything, he asked her if she had thought what it would mean to him. Had she thought of the responsibility he would have to take on, had she thought of the danger she would be putting him in?

"I'll be responsible for myself. And I won't let anybody do him harm."

Margaret shook her head and looked at her husband. "Ruth," he said. His voice was kind, he was being patient. "Ruth, you can't let them or not let them. Don't you know that in our own time a black boy was killed just for talking to a white woman? Dragged from his home and lynched?"

"That was a long time ago, though." She knew the Emmett Till story. Everyone did. "And it didn't happen here. It was Mississippi." Things were different down there.

"When they dragged him out of the river, his eyes were gouged out."

"Don't!"

Margaret said, "Now, James..."

"You ever hear of Brautus Miller? Where did that happen?"

"That was the Kincaid rape. I know about that, but..."

"Now that's it, Ruth. I say Brautus Miller killing, you say Kincaid rape."

"I didn't mean it! I didn't mean that. And it was years and years ago."

"1934. There are people alive now who remember it."

"They were little children then." But Grandma Rose would not have been a child.

"They might have been children, but they remember it. You think the children didn't run along with the mob that tracked him through the woods and beat him to death? Why, Ruth, that was community entertainment."

"They shot him, though, not..."

"Oh yeah, they got around to shooting him. They say they couldn't even carry his body back to town it was so mashed."

"Oh, don't..."

"And there never was a trial. No trial for them and no trial for him. Nobody ever knew if he was the man that did it."

"The girl...the Kincaid girl."

"You think she could tell one nigger from another that night?"

"Don't!" It was the horror but it was the word, too, that she could not bear to hear. "But nothing like that could happen to Wesley. I'll be...We'll be together, we'll be a couple."

"Honey," said Margaret. "That's just the kind of thing that doesn't make any difference to a mob."

"But that was history!" Ruth cried. "We've had civil rights since then, and Martin Luther King and we're almost in another century. Things will never be that bad again!"

James Middlewright laughed at her. It was the same warm laugh she had heard that first day when they sat on the porch and drank tea. He shook his head. "Yes, and we had the Fourteenth Amendment, too. Ruth, don't you think they thought they were right up to date, those killers? And Ruth," he said, "you remember what they did to Martin Luther King?"

Then Wesley came in, hot from running, already speaking as he came through the door, "Sorry. Sorry, I couldn't get away, I meant to be here when..." Then he saw her damp face, engorged with crying and he turned to his parents and said, "You made her cry."

"We should all be cryin' now," said Margaret.

It seemed to go on forever, but Ruth was not even late for work that afternoon. The Middlewrights did not want her, they would not treasure her, and she had always been treasured. But at last they gave up trying to prise her from Wesley. "I think they're hoping one of us will get over it soon," Wesley said. They laughed at the idea that their love was something you could get over. "It's not measles," Ruth said.

They did not give up at home. Ruth knew that they thought they would wear her down if they just kept on. Her mother thought about it all the time and Ruth could tell when she had thought of a new argument; she would say it the first chance she got.

Once she said, "Just suppose you did get married. Just suppose you had a child together. Who would want it? It wouldn't be one thing or the other. Whites wouldn't accept it and Coloreds wouldn't want it either. It would be nobody to anybody."

"It would be beautiful," Ruth said, "and we'd want it." But she guessed that Penny wouldn't. That was what she meant. Ruth thought about the big backyard where she played when she was little, and the tire swing her daddy had tied for her in a tree. That her baby would never swing on. And she wouldn't have cousins to play with. Or he. He wouldn't. She was overwhelmed with grief for the losses her unconceived child was going to have to endure.

Once Penny said, "You know, this is going to kill your Grandma Rose."

Ruth thought it wouldn't. In fact, if it made any difference at all, the crisis seemed to have livened her up a bit. Grandma Rose was an old lady and maybe she hated change, but she liked excitement.

But they were all old. Even her parents were old. They didn't understand the young world and they had forgotten about love and justice both.

Penny was born in the war. They all seemed to be born during wars, her forefathers and foremothers. When Penny was a little girl, there had still been black drinking fountains and white drinking fountains. The bus station still had two fountains. They didn't have the signs on them saying Whites Only and Colored, but you could still see where the signs had been.

Maybe Ruth should have seen it, this stomach-turning race hate they had. She tried to remember when they had shown it, but she could only remember their telling her how bad things used to be and how much better they were now. They didn't have black friends exactly, but they knew black people at work and got along fine with them. They always made the children's black friends welcome. They believed in positive discrimination. They thought people who said "nigger" were low rent. Grandma Rose said it sometimes, casually, as though it were a thing anybody might say. But she had been born before the First World War started in Europe. You couldn't expect more of Grandma Rose. Her parents had been born in the nineteenth century and *their* parents lived in slavery times. Grandma Rose said her grandfather remembered the ragged troops coming home from the Civil War. She was four when America came into what she called the Great War and her father went away to fight and came home safely from Europe and then died of the terrible flu. She was part of the Old South and she thought that Negroes (which she thought was the polite word) had a place and ought to stay in it. And Grandma Daisy, though she was always saying how much younger she was than Rose ("practically another generation!"), was still from that time when white people thought there was something special about being white. Maybe black people did too, Ruth thought, but not anymore. It occurred to her that this was something she and Wesley had never talked about yet.

Once she heard her mother say to her father, "I feel like this is all my fault. I raised her to know no difference." Ruth came into the room then, and Sam didn't answer, but he put his hand over Penny's gently, as though he were forgiving her.

Once her mother said, "You know it says in Deuteronomy, 'Thou shalt not plough with an ass and an ox yoked together...'"

"Well, Mom, which one do you reckon I am?"

"Nor wear garments of divers sorts, as woolen and linen."

"Woolen and linen!"

"And it says in 2 Corinthians, 'Be ye not yoked unequally with unbelievers'."

"But Mom! Wesley *is* a believer!"

"Oh, I know, Ruthie, but you can't take everything literally."

†

She did not feel at home in Wesley's house, but his parents tolerated her presence there and now that school was finished it was almost the only place they could meet. That was how she happened to be there the night they burnt the cross.

In the beginning, it didn't really look like a cross. It was just a whoosh! of flame, sudden and violent against the night sky. They hadn't heard it being lit or constructed. How could they have missed that? Were they so quick, so practiced? So quiet? James started to run toward it, the way you would toward a fire you saw burning near your house. The way anybody would respond to a fire. And then he stopped and walked back to the house and they all came out and stood together on the porch, watching. It burned for a long time, the way a log fire will in the grate. Somebody crossed the lawn and joined them and Ruth looked up to see people standing on all the neighboring porches. A few more came over and all of them were black people. Somebody said, "Have you called the fire department?" and when James said, "No. Let it burn," it confirmed Ruth's feeling that this was not the kind of fire you call the fire department to. Somebody did, though. The engines arrived when the fire was nearly out and the men didn't even unwind the hoses. They could see, she guessed, that they weren't needed now. Or did they like to see it burn? There were eight men, two of them black. Once the flames had stopped shooting upward, you could see the cross shape very clearly, orange against the black sky. Ruth thought of the neon crosses over storefront churches. Jesus Saves, they usually said.

The cross lost its yellow light; its color deepened to red and then to darker red. When it was black, they could see that it was not very tall. Now it looked fragile, burnt through to filigree. Wesley was the first to walk up to it—it was still hot, you could feel the heat of it on your face—and he stood before it for a silent moment, then punched it hard and his knuckles went into the charcoal of it. A chunk fell off. Then somebody else started to hit it. Ruth hardly noticed herself joining them. It was quieter than you would expect. They did not speak and it was silent all around them, except for the glassy sound of the pieces of burnt cross falling on one another. One of the firemen brought a hatchet and they made way for him. When it was nearly leveled, Wesley pulled at the piece that was left in the ground. He had to dig to get a grip on unburnt wood. It had not been planted deep. People stamped on crisp chunks and slivers, reducing them to smaller and smaller pieces. She thought it was like a dance, with the sound of stamping feet for music, and their hard breath. Margaret came with plastic trash sacks and they began to clear up, the way you would after a picnic. When they were done, James shuffled his foot across the ash. "You're gonna have to seed that patch," somebody said to him.

Ruth was shaking, cold to her bones, and Wesley put both his arms around her. She leaned into him, smelling his sweat mixed with the scent of burning. For once they were embracing where they could be seen.

They went indoors, neighbors as well, and the firemen. Half of them had driven away in their engine, but the others came in. Two of the firemen and Ruth were the only white people there. Perhaps there were ten people, or a dozen. Margaret poured out all the coffee in the pot and put more on. The Middlewrights were tee-total, so there was no liquor in the house, but somebody had a fifth of whiskey in his back pocket, and he added it to the cups of those who wanted it. Somebody else went out and came back with a six-pack. It didn't amount to much alcohol, but it seemed like everybody who wanted some had it. Margaret wasn't going to say no tonight.

One of the women looked at Ruth. "Girl, look at your dress!" she said.

Ruth looked down at herself; everyone seemed to be looking at her pale blue summer dress, now covered in soot. "That won't come out," said another woman, her voice sage with knowledge of laundry. Ruth held up her hands. Her knuckles were grained with the stuff and when she licked her lips she could feel grit.

"Well, you surely are a black woman now!" somebody cried, and everybody started to laugh. It wasn't that funny, but they didn't seem to be able to stop. The exhausted little gathering felt like a party, united for a moment in more than fear.

Nobody stayed very long and nobody had much to say. One of the white firemen stood up and thanked Margaret for the coffee, formally, as though she had invited him to a dinner party, and then said to James, "Sir, I sure am sorry this happened." James shook his head and said, "Not your fault."

"I'll take you home," Wesley's father said to her when everybody had left except Margaret's friend from almost next door, who was picking up cups and ferrying them to the sink.

"Oh, it's so late!" she said. With so much to be afraid of, she was suddenly afraid of getting home late.

"Never mind," he said. "I'll say a word." He didn't seem to think there was anything incongruous about his entering Penny and Sam's house and saying a word to them. When she said goodbye to Margaret, Margaret hugged her. That was the first time.

She and Wesley stood beside the car and James said, "Get in. You can ride up front with me." Why was that, she wondered. Maybe he thought it was safer for her to be seen sitting next to a middle-aged black man in the front seat than to a young one in the back.

They drove through familiar streets, which looked strange to her now. The moon had risen and black leaves were warmed in yellow streetlights, chilled in the white light of the moon.

She turned in her seat to look at Wesley. His eyes were bright in the dark. "How did they know?" she asked. "Was it about us?" Neither Wesley nor James answered and she said, "Of course it was."

"I'm afraid it was," James said.

"Oh dear." Who would do it? Who would care? "Was it the Klan?" she asked at last.

James shrugged. "Could have been any stupid cracker," he said. Wesley did not speak.

"I saw them once," she said, "the KKK. They made us laugh, back then." She spoke as though her memory encompassed vanishing decades. It was a parade put on by people, so it was said, from out of state. There had been black people and white standing together on the sidewalk to make fun of the marchers. Nobody had cheered them. They didn't wear white sheets, but brightly colored satin robes—purple, forest green, royal blue, gold—and matching pointed hats that flopped over. They looked like clowns. "We thought they were just stupid," she said. "Ridiculous."

Was it outsiders like them who lit the cross she wondered? It could have been anybody. It could have been people they knew, met every day. Friends. You didn't have to have one of those outfits to do it. But you had to know how, didn't you? How to make a cross?

How to make sure it would stand up? Did they learn it in their Sunday schools when they learned about Easter? They must have painted it all over in kerosene before they put it up. Had it smelled of kerosene? She remembered only the woodfire smell. It could have been a campfire. If she'd been blind, and only felt the heat and smelled the wood, she could have toasted marshmallows on it. Emmett Till had his eyes gouged out of his head.

"Please could I get out a minute," she said.

James looked at her and pulled over to the side of the road at once. She ran to the nearest tree and bent over and retched. Nothing came up, but she stayed bent, coughing and retching and crying. The men stood by the car, leaving her alone. When she came back, she felt as weakened as though she really had thrown up everything that was in her. James handed her a handkerchief. It was huge. She could have used it for a scarf. She wiped her face with it as she got back inside. "Thank you," she said. She half extended it toward him, then thought that it might be better to give it to him washed and ironed. Who would do that? Would Penny wash her daughter's snot and tears out of a black man's handkerchief? She balled it up in her lap.

"Keep that window open," said James. "You're nearly home."

All the lights were on when they pulled up at the McBrides' house, including the porch light. She hesitated. Should she say goodnight now? Thank you for the lift? Wesley still did not speak. She had a sudden tight feeling in her middle, as though all the tubes and hoses that made up her complicated insides were being whipped into hard knots through which nothing could pass, not even breath. Maybe it was going to be too tough for him. Maybe he was deciding whether he dared go on loving her. She was climbing out of the car and looking around at him at the same time, dizzy from twisting and from nearly throwing up.

Sam and Penny must have been waiting just inside the door because they opened it just as James put his foot on the first step. Ruth and Wesley walked behind him. Ruth had her hands clasped in front of her, holding her own hand tight. Wesley reached to her, untangled her fingers, smoothed her palm, brushed her wrist with his fingertips. "Don't you worry," he said. "It's gonna be fine." Her parents were watching James's face for whatever bad news it held.

James began to speak as soon as they were indoors, before anybody would have had a chance to welcome him or to ask him to sit down. If anyone were going to do that. "Good evenin'," he said, and he told them his name and nodded toward Wesley, who stood back a little.

Ruth had begun to step forward without letting him go, so that their clasped hands between their extended arms were like a knot in a string.

"I believe you've met my boy Wesley Adam before." Ruth looked at Wesley's face as she moved back toward him. She hadn't known his middle name.

Penny nodded quickly. Ruth thought that she looked a little ashamed. Well, she ought to, she thought.

"I'm sorry to bring your Ruth home so late," James went on. "Only we've had a little trouble at our place and it was hard to get away."

"Trouble!" Her mother cried out that terrible word as though it might mean anything and Ruth ran to her.

"I'm fine," she said. "I'm absolutely fine."

"Mr. Middlewright," her father said, "Please do sit down. Can I get you some coffee? Or somethin' cold?" A little pause. "And Wesley?"

James sat on the sofa. "Thank you," he said, "but I think I'm about coffee-ed out," and he smiled.

Everyone sat down. The two fathers were on the sofa and Wesley and Penny in the chairs. Ruth pulled out the piano stool.

It was Wesley who began. "Somebody burned a cross in our front yard tonight," he said.

"Oh, my God!"

"They sneaked up in the dark..." He was going on, but his voice was shaking. He faltered and stopped.

James told the story of the evening. There wasn't much to tell, but he told them all of it so that there was nothing they were left not knowing: the sudden discovery, the fireman, the neighbors coming, the gathering afterward in the kitchen. He told them that there had been no damage. "Nothin' worse than a patch on my lawn," he said, "and that's a mess most years anyway."

Ruth's parents, who had been silent while James spoke, now seemed to be saying everything at once. "I'm sorry you had that happen," and "How is your wife taking it?" and "Somebody could have been killed." "Who would do such a thing?" and "Do you have any idea who it was?" but finally Ruth's mother said to her, "This is the kind of thing that happens when you..." She trailed off and

Ruth didn't know if it was because she thought the rest of her sentence was obvious or because she got embarrassed by it.

"It surely is," said James, "and I don't know who it was, but I am afraid our children have been noticed."

"Who…?" escaped Ruth.

"Have you been goin' around together in town?" Penny asked.

"But I've never heard of anything like this around here," said Sam. "Not in my time."

"Maybe nobody provoked them before," Penny said.

"It's not our fault," said Wesley. "It's their fault, whoever they are."

He was going to say more, but James spoke first. "I guess we all need to decide what's to be done next," he said, "and maybe," rising from the settee, "the middle of the night isn't the time to do it."

"Of course, you'll want to get back to Mrs. Middlewright," said Penny, who seemed, Ruth thought, not able to settle on an attitude. She suddenly thought of Margaret alone in the house with the burnt-black grass outside.

When the door had closed behind them, Ruth reflected that James had been the only one who acted like he knew how to behave.

"I don't think it's so smart for you two to be all over each other like you do in public," Penny said.

"We were just holding hands!" Ruth was outraged at the injustice. "Barely!"

"Well, it sure was enough for somebody," Penny answered.

"Oh, and you think they were right," Ruth said, ready for the fight now.

"I'm goin' to bed," Sam told them, and started turning off lights.

"But don't you want to talk about this?"

"No baby, I surely do not. Your friend JM said it right. This ain't for the middle of the night."

"Why do you call him that?" Penny asked. "You don't know him, do you?"

"Oh, hell no. I don't know him to talk to, but I know who he is. He works down at the Manglefords plant. He's some kind of a chemist. I'm goin' to bed."

Ruth expected to lie awake all night arguing in her head with her parents, but she fell asleep right away. She had just time to wonder whether it might not turn out to have been a good thing, that cross. JM had said "our children."

†

Ruth was ready for a big conference with all the parents and all the brothers—except maybe for Wesley's little brother, who was only ten. But there never was one. They talked on the phone or had meetings she didn't know were happening. No one told her when they finally gave up, when they stopped deciding how to pull them apart and started deciding how to send them away, but one evening her brother Amos telephoned from Ohio where he was working and said, "So, I hear you're moving to California." It was the first she had heard of it.

She and Wesley had both gone on as though they were entering university in the fall. A part of her, that part which wasn't longing to explode the world she had grown up in, wished that she could go to college like anybody else and have a boyfriend that she saw some weekends and over the holidays, and wrote love letters to and saved money with and got married to when they both had degrees. It might be better at college. Students were more sophisticated, more daring.

But somebody in Elder Springs wanted to kill her. Or wanted to kill Wesley and save her from him and his blackness, which was worse. A woman she hardly knew came up to her in Bumgartners, where she was trying out pens, and said, "I don't care how much you think you love him, I don't see how anybody could do such a thing to her mother."

"I..." She had so much to say that she couldn't get anything out and she just watched as the woman walked off, unanswered, swaggering, Ruth thought, as though she had done something clever.

She tried to be comfortable in her home, feeling as though her family were in its end times. But it was too hard. It was as though she had not just done a bad thing, but become a bad person. The people who had always loved her best could not even bear to look at her now.

"Mom," she said one evening, capturing her mother as she walked past Ruth's open bedroom door. "You know I haven't ever done anything so bad. I never smoked dope (hardly, she reserved to herself) and I never smuggled liquor into a party and I never..." she hesitated, trying to think how she might decently assert her decency. "Mom, do you know I'm a virgin? I'm practically the only virgin I know. Except for Miranda." Miranda was Penny's great-niece. She was only ten months old. Mentioning her was a kind of desperate joke and had probably been a mistake. "Mom, I've always done right, as much as I could. You know I've tried. This is the first thing I've ever done you really didn't like."

"Well, you saved up for a good 'un."

Ruth never found out exactly why her brothers had California in their minds before they dropped it into hers, but as the summer weeks passed, California came to be accepted as their inevitable destination. "It's about as far as they could send us," Wesley said. "Next stop, Japan."

They didn't have to go; they could stay and tough it out. They could overcome. But in the end they decided to take their banishment as a blessing. They would leave the Garden, like Adam and Eve, and eat their bread by the sweat of their brow like grown-ups. They might move on to Japan one day, who knows? No one would burn any more crosses on their parents' lawns, anyway.

Paul and Jasmine were married on Labor Day Weekend. "Maybe it would be better if I'm not a bridesmaid, after all," Ruth told Jasmine.

Jasmine said, "Oh, Ruth, of course you have to be in my wedding. Of course you do!"

Besides, Ruth thought, the pale yellow dresses had been made to measure. "Is Wesley invited?" she asked. It was hard, but whoever said yes to her had to say yes to them both.

Jasmine's good manners allowed only a breath before she answered. "You bring any guest you like."

When Ruth asked him, Wesley said, "Maybe best if I don't," and she looked away from him, ashamed.

Ruth and Wesley were going to get married in California. The parents all agreed that it would just be asking for trouble to have a wedding like theirs in Elder Springs. Margaret had known the pastor of the Baptist church of Bitterwater before he went out there.

"We're going to a place called Bitterwater?" But Margaret said, "It's only a name. They say it's a pretty place."

Bitterwater wasn't far away from San Francisco, near Salinas. It was close to the sea, to Berkley, to universities, places to work, places where an interracial couple could live. There was that name for what they were.

Ruth didn't envy Jasmine her beautiful wedding. When she was a little girl she had imagined layers of petticoats and piles of presents, but she didn't care about any of that now. She hadn't known what she thought a wedding was, but now she thought it ought to be like being lifted up in loving hands and handed into a little boat, and tenderly urged from the bank until the stream took you and you moved into your new life like a leaf on the water. Well, she was going to have to scramble in on her own. She and Wesley would just shove each other in, that was all there was to it.

Ruth wanted to travel on a train, but Amtrak was too expensive, so they went to Charlotte and caught a plane. The two sets of parents drove their children separately to the airport, where they caught the same plane. The black parents and the white parents stood beside each other at the departure gate and waved goodbye to them. Loving hands waving, each to its own child.

They were married on the seventeenth of September, which was a Thursday. Margaret flew out to be there; she brought Wesley's brother Matthew with her. Matthew loved California and said he was going to live there when he grew up and could he visit at Christmas? James wished he could come. He couldn't get away but he sent his love and a camera "for your memories to come." Penny wrote a long letter that she folded into the silver and white wedding card she sent, and she and Sam sent a check. On the card, under the printed message, she had written, "Love you forever," and they had both signed it.

That night Ruth telephoned Penny and told her all about the day. She has phoned her mother every Thursday night since then.

Personal Storage

I will say to my soul,
Soul, thou hast much goods laid up for many years;
take thine ease, eat, drink, and be merry.

—Luke 12:19

It was Sunday morning. Warm autumn weather sat on the low hills of North Carolina; sunshine poured through clear windows and lay thick as butter on the wooden floor and the wooden table and caressed the shoulders of every single member of the Sunday school class and Bible study group at Calvary Hope Baptist Church. And mine too.

The wave of prayers and petitions came round the table, sweeping toward me. It was moving, and surprising, how much people were able to say, how much sorrow they dared expose. The young man across from me lifted a scared face when it was his turn. "My sister's new baby's got two holes in her heart," he said. "They're going to operate Tuesday in Raleigh. The hospital in Raleigh." I tried to imagine a newborn heart. It would be a giblet, I thought. How could you operate on something the size of your thumb? "Heal her, Lord, if it be your will," somebody said, and the others said amen. I said amen. Frank Thomas, our brother in Christ, had been diagnosed with cancer and we asked God to give him and Sally, his wife, the strength to bear this trial. One seat closer and a woman led us in giving thanks for the safety of her Latino husband, sitting beside her now. What perils had he endured to make his safety something to pray about? Everyone in the room knew but me. Then it was her husband's turn. He speaks English, I was told, but he prays in Spanish. "He's praying for his family he had to leave back home in Honduras," his wife told us. I was caught by that 'had to' and also by his being Honduran. Most of the new Latino citizens of the town were Guatemalan, I thought. She went on: "...and thankin' God for his good new Christian friends, and for bringin' him to the Lord Jesus." Everyone said amen as he lifted his head and smiled around the circle. What was he before he was a Christian, I wondered. I'm supposed to be an anthropologist; surely I should know what they worship in Honduras. Later I asked and was told that he used to be a Catholic. We asked God's blessing on Edith, whose husband had come home for two nights and then gone off again. "It's so hard for her, Lord," Edith's sister said, "bringin' up that child by herself, and she can't depend on anybody in this world but You." We said amen, though everyone knew that her mother was a rock from which no storm could sweep her. "I just pray you make her faith strong enough to hold up under so many blows," her sister went on. No one was impatient as her prayer became narrative, explanatory. Someone passed her a handful of Kleenex. Amen. Amen. We prayed for the continuing recovery of Miss Villard, who was doing so well after her slight stroke. We thanked God that I was among them. We thanked God for the kind welcome I, a stranger, had received from them. Someone invited our prayers for the preacher, who was not really well enough to work, but who kept working. "It sounds to me like walkin' pneumonia," someone said. There was general concern for him. "He just keeps givin' of himself." Then the circle was closed and we came back to Ben, the leader of the class.

Now that the opening prayers were done, it was time for our lesson. Ben was using a book of lessons, one appointed for each Sunday in the year. That day we were to consider giving. "A new initiative," he explained, "in our cooperative program."

I knew something about cooperative giving because I had interviewed the director of the regional Baptist association and he had told me how it worked. He made sure I understood: voluntary contributions, not dues. "It's the way to do great things with little gifts."

The new initiative in giving encouraged us to give a bit more, if we could.

The lesson included a little didactic play, which we were to read out. There were only two parts and I was given one. I was Marie.

The play is set in an unspecified foreign country that has an unfair criminal justice system. It does not take place in the United States. My friend—that is, Marie's friend—has been arrested and locked up, and he has to stay there until he has paid a certain amount of money. There is no one but Marie to pay his fine and buy his freedom. I am willing to help. I send money every single day, but it isn't doing any good. The debt does not diminish. The dialogue begins. I am talking to another friend; Michael, he's called. The young man whose sister had the sick newborn plays Michael. He explains to me (to Marie) that interest is being added to the fine every day; the amount I am paying will never overtake the debt. Marie needs to have things explained to her, I thought. He says that I'll have to give more. I cannot afford it, my lines say. I have to live too, after all. I'm doing the best I can. I read with expression and so does the young man. We throw ourselves into our parts. "But Marie..." he protests. Then Michael has an idea. "Wait! You send the money in every day in the mail. If you carried it in by hand instead, you could save the cost of the stamp and add that to the money for the fine. You could double what you pay and you could get him out!" But no, I will not do that. I don't have the time. I can't make that long journey so often. I have other things to do.

I (not Marie, but me) thought, Why doesn't she put all the money aside and post it just once a week, then. That would cut the postage to a seventh, or a sixth, anyway. And what's wrong with Michael's helping? And how big a fine can it be if the price of a postage stamp is a significant contribution? But I was taking it too literally. It was only a little instructive tale. It wasn't about the best way to pay off debts or to explore gender politics or anybody's psychology, much less the politics of foreign dictatorships.

Marie's friend languishes in prison because she will not do enough. Are we, Ben asked us, doing enough for Christ where we find him in our fellow human beings? Do we see him naked and clothe him, sick and visit him, in prison and bring him comfort? That was the meaning of the play. That was the meaning of Marie's obtuseness, her stubbornness. It was all our stubbornness. Like Marie, we weren't doing enough.

We moved then to the Bible. Our text was the story of the Rich Young Ruler. It appears in three of the gospels. My friend Gloria, who brought me here, read out Luke's version:

And a certain ruler asked him, saying Good Master, what shall I do to inherit eternal life? And Jesus said unto him, Why callest thou me good? None is good, save one, that is God. Thou knowest the commandments, Do not commit adultery, Do not kill, Do not steal, Do not bear false witness, Honor thy father and thy mother. And he said, All these have I kept from my youth up. Now when Jesus heard these things, he said unto him, Yet lackest thou one thing: sell all that thou hast, and distribute unto the poor, and thou shalt have treasure in heaven: and come, follow me. And when he heard this, he was very sorrowful: for he was very rich.

There was a general chuckle at the plight of the rich young ruler. Somebody said, "I just bet he was sorrowful!" It was more or less what they expected of rich people, I guessed. Ben expounded the point of the text. "Now, that's not a commandment for everybody," he began, "but we should all be *prepared* to give up everything and follow Christ if that commandment ever comes to us." He went on. "Now, I know some of you feel like you're giving all you can, and maybe you won't be able to do any more for this new initiative, and I appreciate that. But it isn't just giving we're talking about here, but it's *sacrificial* giving."

He paused, giving us a moment to take in what he had said. "Let me tell you a story about this lady that came in to the Farm Home Administration—you know, I work down there." He glanced at me, the only one present who might not know.

There was a kind of stir around the table, a renewal of attention. Everyone settled to hear the story.

"She told us," Ben said, "she was gonna lose her home. It was ready to be repossessed. I said that well, we might could help her. If she could pay just a part of her debt. If she can't make the regular interest we can come in with cheap credit. That's what we're there for." He looked around the circle, his face intent.

I imagined him in his office, just so intent. I imagined him looking up, rising, welcoming the woman, regarding her with that same earnest look.

I can see Ben. He would smile at the woman, invite her in.

"Please sit down," he says. But she stands just inside the door, frowning and uncertain. She looks as though she could as easily back herself out as come any farther in. He indicates the chair across the desk from his, but she stands still. She looked at him briefly when she came in, but now her glance slides over him and makes its way around the room, jumping urgently from one point to another as though it might encounter something hidden and malign anywhere in Ben's plain, pleasant little office.

He walks around the desk and over to her. It takes only a few steps to reach her. "Please do sit down," he says again. He touches the sleeve of her sweater, just at the elbow where her arm is bent to hold her carryall and her purse close to her body, and guides her to the chair. His fingers just barely rest on the heather-sage wool. He and the woman finally reach her chair and with his other hand he pulls it out a little further. Warily, she sits.

She perches tensely, as though she might spring up in an instant. For a moment, his hands are poised as though he has just balanced her on a narrow shelf and is waiting to see whether she will settle or fall, but then he leaves her and goes back to his own side of the desk. Carefully, matching her care, he sits down, picks up a pencil and addresses her:

"How can we help?" he asks.

Now she looks at him and he sees that she is not as old as he thought. Perhaps forty-something; maybe nearer fifty than forty. It was her look of weary anxiety that made her look so old. It is a look he recognizes. He has not seen this woman before, but he has seen that look before.

He knows better than to ask again yet. He sits and waits. He smiles a little, not so much that he looks as though he's laughing at her or is too cheerful when she is so sad, but enough so that he won't come across as stern. People get afraid in offices. It's delicate. Some things you can only learn from experience.

Finally she speaks, "I think I'm in trouble."

"Well now, why don't you tell me about it?" he says.

"Thank you. I will. I will tell you." Yet still she pauses.

He waits, deferential. It is hard, he knows, to come in and talk to somebody, especially somebody younger than you, about something personal. Some people think a thing has to be medical or sexual to be personal. He knows better. Nothing is more personal than money.

"I'm afraid I'm goin' to lose my home!" Her voice rises in pitch. It wavers.

"Well now, we'll just see if we can't keep that from happening," he says.

There are tears there, but they do not fall. The concentration with which she keeps them back is terrible to see. "It's my mortgage," she begins when she can speak. "My husband used to pay some toward it ever' month, but this last year I've had it all to do, and it's just got a little behind and a little behind and now I'm so far behind, I just don't think there's any way I can catch up. Or I could if I had more time, but now they come to tell me that I've only got two months to pay off the whole thing—the whole arrears—and you know there's just no way in the world I could do that. I don't make enough in two months to pay all that even if I give up eatin'. All the growin' land's gone already and if they take my home…if they take my home away from me, I just don't know what I will do. I'll just be livin' like a dog."

He doesn't interrupt her, but when she has finished this, her grief's first outpouring, he says gently, "Now you say your husband...?" This is another part that's delicate. You can't come out and ask if he's dead, and you can't ask if he's gone and run off. But you need to know whether there might be another income to be considered. If you leave the phrase hanging just unfinished, the client will usually say, "...died last spring," or "...high tailed it out of here as soon as it looked like he might have to do some work." Or something.

This lady says, "What about him?" The threat of tears is gone.

"Can he help?"

"He's dead," she says. Her voice falls to a heavy stop.

Ben says, "Well, I'm real sorry to hear that." He pauses. "Your mortgage must have been insured."

She looks away from him, not searching anxiously for phantoms now, but fixing her gaze somewhere else. "His name wasn't on the mortgage," she says, "so it didn't make no difference when he died. I had that plot before I ever got married. I was born in that house. My daddy was a renter and I decided I would never die in a rented room."

Ben half turns to his computer. "Well, let's start with your whole name," he says.

I heard Ben's real voice. It drowned out his daydream voice and I admonished myself for my moonshine. That woman could have had any one of a hundred stories, stories so strange I could not think of them at all. Perhaps she did have a husband all the time, bedridden or hung over, or just out of work, or working hard but making less than the minimum wage. Ben hadn't said. That was not part of the story he was telling. It wasn't the point. Maybe there were children somewhere. Perhaps she had never been married. Maybe she had inherited the house entire and had mortgaged it to finance some ill-advised business venture that had failed years ago.

Ben was saying, "I said we could help her. I was real glad to be able to offer her some hope. Only I said, you're still going to have to pay something toward the arrears and then something every month, and keep those payments up. Only they'll be a lot smaller than what you're having to pay now. Well, she said she just couldn't do it. I kept figuring and figuring and we kept making the payment smaller and smaller, but no matter how little it was she was going to have to pay, she'd say no, she couldn't do it. She didn't have much, but she did have some money coming in, and still she didn't have a dime to pay toward saving that property.

"Then come to find out she was renting three storage facilities and all of them full of stuff. I said to her, You'd be better off having a yard sale—that way at least you'd get something out of all that stuff. You'd even be better giving it away! She could save enough in three months to pay what the Farm Home Administration wanted her to put in against the arrears. She was paying three hundred and fifty dollars a month."

The amount was climactic. It brought a gasp or a sigh from the listeners. Breath in or breath out. How could she? Someone said, "It breaks your heart to think of it." I wondered, what could she be keeping that she cannot part with, even at such a price?

Her voice sounded in my mind like a memory, as though I had heard it before and was hearing it now. That high, clear, mountain voice, sharpened by pain, pointed by grievance. She was talking to me, or maybe to herself.

"'Course there's the furniture," that voice said, plangent, full of echoes. "Those big pieces that belonged to Mother. People don't appreciate craftsmanship like that any more. There was that woman lived on Catawba Avenue—Bindle, her name was, or Bobbin, somethin' that makes you think of the mills. All closed now, the cloth mills. Taken over by the big northern companies and then run down to nothin'. That woman—her name was Harben, I remember it now—she sold all her beautiful furniture that she'd got from her mother and daddy to that swindler Poteat, and bought a whole lot of flimsy factory-made stuff from him. Formica and plywood. For near enough the same price. It was just about a straight swap. And she thought she'd done well for herself. They don't appreciate… Poteat knew what he'd got, even if she didn't know what she'd parted with. I went round to his store and looked at it. Well, there might have been somethin' I could 'a used. It was beautiful wood they used in the old days. Not just oak, but elm, too, and walnut, and there was a table that had a border of birdseye maple, just as pretty as if somebody'd embroidered it with a needle. 'Oh, this is a antique,' is what he said. A antique, my foot! He probably told Miz Harben that same table was way too big and heavy. 'Nobody wants this big ol' stuff these days. I can't hardly sell it.' I've heard the way they talk. Furniture men. Then once he got on the other end, it was a antique and he was askin' five times as much. Ten times. Hell, you could buy a dozen a those Formica tables for what he wanted for that pretty thing. It's enough to make you cuss.

"I can remember my sweet mother sittin' in the big rocker. That's why I went in my own space at the storage facility and cleared everything off it. So I can sit in it and rock. It creaks, but it's still solid. They keep things nice there; there's not a whiff of damp nor a spot of mildew on anything. And it's quiet. Nobody bothers you.

"It was always a popular pattern. They've started makin' rockin' chairs like that again, with that slick curve to the rockers that makes 'em look like the runners on a sleigh, and arms that curve down under your hand like the head on a fiddle. But they're Reproduction. Heritage. You might just as well get a rocker in pieces in a cardboard box down to Perkins Hardware and sit in it and look at a picture of an old one as waste your money on one of those Colonial Style frauds. Mother's was the real thing. But everything about her was real. My mother couldn't tell a lie to save her life. Not ever'body liked it, but that's how she was. She was a real mother, too. She had to do outside work sometimes but she was our mother every hour she lived. 'Her children arise up and call her blessed,' and that's the truth.

"I'm fixin' to bring it home before much longer, her rocker. Once I've got the place done up like it used to be. Once I'm sure where it'll sit. And the oak dining room suit, and Daddy's bookcase. That's solid walnut, I think. I'll polish them with real beeswax polish and bring out the light in the wood. You can't do much better than dust in here.

"I've got two real nice dressers, too, and the cedar chest—they all take up a good deal of room. But most of what I got down there to Personal Storage Inc. is papers. All packed in cardboard boxes. Now, they look neat from the outside, but they need sorting out badly. One day, when I've got the time, I'll go through them. Why, they're more valuable even than the furniture! They're real history! All the family papers—they go right back to the War Between the States and some of 'em further back than that even. The old family Bible is in one of them boxes. I can't say just which one, but I'll find it right away, once I start opening them. Of course I've got my Bible at the house for readin', but the big leather bound one with all the entries of births and deaths in it, that's important. A document. It's too precious to leave layin' around the house, the state it's in now. I'll have a little table for it, just the right size, when I bring it home. My daddy showed me—it was before I could even read—my own name in that book, Martha Mary Stanton Woodbury, right where he wrote it hisself, the day I was born.

"And letters. There's letters goin' right back to the war, when my daddy was overseas. Before I was born. Letters from both my grandmothers. You could put those in a book. They make books nowadays out of old letters. They're history. And I think there might be a diary in there, that my mother kept when she was a girl. Lord! That would be the Great Depression time. The time between the wars. Now, anybody would be interested in that. Papers like that are valuable. And there are pictures, boxes and boxes of photos, some of them in real nice old frames. And whole newspapers with important stories: D-Day and the Kennedy assassination and that flood in '77 or '78 when the bridge was washed away. Besides all the ones with the family in them: weddings and retirements and church news, and Mother cut out the clipping whenever I won a prize for anything. I would've done that myself if the Lord had blessed me with children that had a' lived. But their birth announcements are in there: To Robert and Martha Gimpsey a Son, To Robert and Martha Gimpsey a Daughter. And their death announcements are there. A birth and then a death, a birth and then a death. Deeply mourned by sorrowing parents. They never got old enough to be baptized. But that don't matter. The Lord loved them, and they're with Him now. They were budded on earth to bloom in heaven. Beautiful flowers in the Master's bouquet. And I have all the cards; my birthday cards from when I was a little girl, and then—I shouldn't wonder if they was in the same box—all the congratulations cards for the babies. The tags off all the wedding presents. Sympathy cards for the babies, and the ones for Daddy, and for Mother. The ones I got when Bob died are still there on the mantelpiece. I hadn't but just started renting the facility when he was taken. I'll have to get round to puttin' them in a box and fetchin' them down to the storage. I'll do that real soon."

Martha's voice, so strong and resonant, faded. It could be something different altogether, I told myself, that she had in storage. But whatever it was, it was precious to her. I had a sort of sense, as Ben's voice supplanted Martha's in my head, how it would be to have him tell me to put my treasures into a yard sale, to spread them out on trestle tables for strangers to pick through. I wondered if I would be any more sensible, any more tough-minded, than Ben's much-pitied client.

"But you know," Ben was saying. The story was ending now. "She just couldn't do it. And I told her, you'll lose all that stuff anyway. It'll be taken away from you. Your creditors will take it if your house gets repossessed. But that woman could not bear to part with her possessions. She was just not free of those things."

He was silent for a moment, looking around at us; that was the way he did it, I realized. The way he invited us to ponder his message. He gave us the story, then gave us the time to encompass it in silence. Then he told us. He said, "Are we free of our possessions? Just like that woman, are we putting everything at risk just because we can't bear to give up warehouses full of things we don't even have a use for? Maybe our eternal souls are in danger of being repossessed, even though Christ is standing ready to pay every debt and set us free. We might be like that Rich Young Ruler and just like him we can't truly follow Christ because it makes us too sorrowful to give up our many possessions. We would be better off if we were to sell all our worldly ambitions or give them away and then invest everything in our salvation instead, and our eternal home."

We sat quiet, reflecting. Everybody looked thoughtful. Perhaps they were shamed, realizing their worldliness. I thought what a good story that was, a little modern parable: firmly linked to the Bible text, impelling consideration. Really a lot like Jesus's parables. It was local and the situation was recognizable, it invited sympathy for its protagonist while still allowing us to know better. And the moral was clear. Better than the Bible story perhaps for us who don't know any rich young rulers but who have had some experience of unprofitably hanging on to things.

And then there was Ben, whom I had misjudged. I didn't notice until now that I was misjudging him, but I was. Here was Ben, not a religious professional, following his timetable, working his way week by week through mass-produced, mass distributed inspiration, ploddingly selling virtue to people who were mildly in the market for it, making a pitch for piety and good causes. His was a small town life, closed in by mountains, restricted by small expectations and tethered by responsibilities.

But all the time, while he did his full-time job and his part-time duty to the church, while he fathered his family and helped his parents out, he had been carrying with him the texts of his faith, making his life into a text. Here was this window he knew how to open in his small town sky, a window through which great truths were to be seen. He showed us the view, gestured to it: "Look! Here is the kingdom of heaven!" His vision had seemed narrow to me, but that was because I did not see it with his eyes. Really, from time to time, the sky opens wide at his touch, and beyond it is eternity.

A Moment of Rapture

*Then we which are alive and remain shall be caught
up together with them in the clouds,
to meet the Lord in the air: and so shall we ever be
with the Lord.
Wherefore comfort one another with these words.*
—I Thessalonians 4:17

The dogs had been barking for a good two hours since Jeff started listening. Who knows how long before that. Sounds didn't leak into the house. Jeff and Laurel always went to bed with the windows and doors closed and locked. Closed for the air conditioning. Locked for security. But tonight had been so balmy, so full of smells and summer sounds, that Jeff had hesitated when they came indoors. He had a sense that in a minute he would remember something, recognize something not quite forgotten. But there was only the soft heavy air and the smell of grass. So he said, "It's a nice night," and Laurel had agreed and they had come in and shut the door behind them. He made sure the windows were closed (for the air conditioning) and locked (for security) in his son Alan's room. Laurel checked those in Peter's. Then they said their short separate prayers and went to bed.

They kissed each other goodnight and lay under just a sheet, apart, hands touching. The air conditioning was working; he could hear the hum of it as it passed the air through its entrails and blew it out softly—cooled, dehumidified, and ionized—but still it seemed hot. He fell asleep, listening to his wife's breathing, familiar as his own, and to the unobtrusive breath of the Central Air.

When he awoke, he thought it must be nearly morning. He had been deeply asleep, dreaming of something vanished now. He listened intently for the boys but they had not wakened yet. He looked at the clock. Eleven forty. Funny how that happened sometimes; he had been sleeping for seven minutes.

He would not sleep again now, he thought. The air felt stale, sickly, as though it had been too often breathed. It didn't smell bad, exactly, just overused. He got up quietly, so he wouldn't wake Laurel, and went to the window. As he started to lift it, the frame caught a little and scraped. At the noise, Laurel turned. He waited, watching her. She opened her eyes and looked at him, clouded, confused by this early awakening.

"What time is it?"

"Night time," he said. They were both whispering, though the boys couldn't have heard them from their rooms. "I'm sorry. Go back to sleep."

She frowned.

"Thought I'd let some air in," he said.

"Good idea." She turned over, moving just enough so that her head made a new hollow in her pillow and, so far as he could see, she fell asleep at once.

He turned back to the window and opened it fully. The frame ground against the sash and he resolved to plane it. Or grease it somehow; soap… candle wax. The trouble was, opening them so seldom, you just assumed they were in good shape. He should do regular checks, just to make sure, to keep ahead of things.

Once his window stood open and had stopped protesting, he heard the barking. Someone moving past, he thought. Dogs'll do that. Even a friend, if they turn up at night, will set them off. And a good thing. Security. It sounded like two dogs. He went into the living room where he hesitated for a moment. These were both big windows. And they were close to the floor. A person could climb in and you'd never hear them, not if you were asleep in the other room. And if there was a prowler around… No reason there should be. Only the dogs were still barking. He'd thought they would quiet down when whoever it was got beyond their boundary. Man, they were loud dogs!

Still he hesitated, his hands on the window locks. But somehow, having come into his own living room to open his own windows to let fresh air in, he could not bring himself to leave the locks on. What kind of a man, what kind of a father or a husband, could be afraid to open his windows to the summer air?

These windows ran much smoother and the first one slid upward at his first urging as though it had its own reasons.

He could distinguish their two voices clearly now. One was high-pitched, not yappy like a little dog, no. Full, but kind of screamish; it finished sometimes on what was almost a howl. The other one was deep timbered; the barking started as a rumble in its throat, then ran out like a holler. He imagined the dog: black and brindled, a big squat beast with a square muzzle and short legs. Old. Grey hairs behind his nose and growing out of his ears. Worse tempered now than when he was young.

The noise was coming from the next house along—the direction was clear now—so why didn't he remember ever seeing these animals? Maybe whoever owned the dogs kept them penned in the day. Maybe he took them to work with him. Stupid thing to do, if he did. Brutes like that.

Jeff went back to bed. He pulled his pajamas off and pushed them away with his feet. He didn't feel any cooler. Anyway, didn't staying covered keep the heat off you? All those Arabs and Bedouins in The Holy Land wearing their long cotton gowns in the desert. But maybe that was just against the sun. They wore business suits now, didn't they, but they had those black and white bandannas. Through the open windows he could hear, in the brief pauses between barks, the chirruping of cicadas or grasshoppers or whatever insects they were that sang in the short summer nights. Playing fiddles, he thought, instead of storing food for the winter. That was a fable. He remembered being told it when he was hardly more than a baby, when he was first at school. Who was it that stored up the food? Bees, maybe. Or ants. Yes, he thought it was ants. Funny kind of a story to tell kids, if you wanted them to learn it was better to work hard than to spend your time tomcattin' around. Nobody liked ants. Grasshoppers could do a lot of damage—well, locusts could, anyway, and they were some kind of kin to grasshoppers— but just the same, there was something about them, to a child. Leaping up out of the long grass like they did, the same color as the grass, life in the still summer meadows. Who would you rather be like? None of the kids he knew would rather be a farmer than a fiddler. They knew too much about farming.

He'd taken that story home to tell his mama and she'd said it was just like the wise and the foolish virgins. He hadn't known what a virgin was—except for "yon virgin" in the Christmas carol, which couldn't have anything to do with the grasshoppers because, for one thing, Christmas happened in the winter when all the grasshoppers were gone; dead or sleeping, he hadn't known then which it was and he realized he still didn't—and when he'd asked Mama, she'd said it was what they called a girl in olden times. And she'd taken him to her big chair under the lamp and picked up her Bible off the little table and read him Matthew 25:1-12, where it says that the Kingdom of Heaven is like ten virgins. It was a confusing story then; there were so many virgins, and only one bridegroom. It had made him think of hens around a rooster, more than the kingdom of God. But he couldn't have been more than five years old. Younger than Peter was now. But Mama was right about the grasshopper and the virgins. It was the same lesson. Not everybody would have thought of that. She was a smart woman, and she was a good Christian mother: she found lessons everywhere, found a gentle rein in everything to pull her children toward the Lord. When the grasshopper feels the cold coming on, and he's only wearing his embroidered vest (he hadn't known he remembered so much of it), and he doesn't have any work clothes, any warm clothes, then he knows. He knows he's left it too late. All the harvest he should have gathered in is gathered already, by others, or dead from an early frost. He knows now that he's going to starve if he doesn't freeze first, so he goes to the ants and the chief ant tells him he should have thought of that before. There isn't enough to go around. And that's what the wise virgins say to the foolish virgins, too, when the bridegroom turns up in the middle of the night and they've used up all their oil so they can't light their lamps. There isn't enough to go round, so the foolish virgins have to go buy some more and when they get back the door is shut and they knock on it and pound on it and the bridegroom says, "Verily, I know you not." The bridegroom was a figure of Jesus, he learned. He never confessed it, but it seemed spiteful to him for the girls not to share their oil, and make the other ones miss their wedding. And not so merciful of the bridegroom to shut the door on them. Just like he'd hated the head ant for being so self-satisfied. But that wasn't the lesson. The lesson was to be always ready. The lesson was not to wait until the last minute to get yourself right.

He had almost fallen asleep a couple of times, but he was moving further and further from sleep now. It was like when the boys were babies—especially Peter, he thought—and wouldn't settle to sleep. He'd wake up hearing a whimper and listen to it growing to a wide-awake complaint, and still he'd think, maybe he'll go back to sleep by himself. Maybe he'll drop off. It was easy to forget, now that they lowered themselves into sleep as though it were a pool, throwing their solid little bodies into ever more extravagant postures, so that sometimes they had almost to be unwrapped from their bedclothes, without ever surfacing into consciousness until morning. Sometimes, now that they were such accomplished, such dedicated sleepers, it was hard to remember how hard-won their naps had been when they were small, how tired their parents were all the time. It was worse for Laurel, of course, but sometimes when he set off for work in the morning, gritty-eyed with fatigue, he had thought that he would give anything in the world for an uninterrupted night. So in the middle of the night he would cling to sleep, hoping that Peter would drift again into a quiet doze, even for an hour, even half an hour. He was ashamed to remember it, but he had probably prayed more often and more fervently for Peter to go back to sleep than he had for anything else in his life. He shifted in his bed now, listening to the dogs as he used to listen to Peter. Between outbursts he drifted, dreaming that he was asleep. A moment's silence and he started counting seconds, nearly holding his breath. There... they had stopped barking. In his dream, Peter was not sleeping, only gathering breath for the next insistent shout, outraged and grief-laden. The child-rearing book in which they— young parents, just learning—had put their faith said that you had to leave them to get through the night or they'd never learn, and Jeff's mother said the same thing: pick that baby up whenever he cries, she had assured them, and you'll be making a rod for your own back. So he and Laurel would lie stiffly in their bed, willing the small, tyrannical voice to release them, wondering which of them would be the first to break, who would have to stride into the next room and pick up the shuddering child, hot and pink from crying, sobbing reproachfully into your shoulder, damp with tears and drool. Usually it was Jeff.

He looked at his clock. Nearly one.

Well, these dogs weren't going to quit. They were set for the night. And so was he. Funny that Laurel could sleep through it. Well, he couldn't stand it. He wouldn't stand it. Carefully, he slipped himself out of the bed, making as little disturbance as he could. He felt for his discarded pajama bottoms, and Laurel shifted and sighed in her sleep. He stopped and waited until she was still, then he went out into the hall. He looked in on the boys. They were deeply asleep. Well, he thought, they were on the quiet side of the house—away from the dogs.

He unlocked the back door and put on an old raincoat that was hanging on the peg beside it. Underneath the row of gardening sweaters, padded jackets for backyard cold weather, forgotten plastic coats and ancient capes, stood their collection of outdoor footwear. He put his feet into a pair of rubber boots, feeling garden grit in his bed-warm, night-softened feet. He closed the door behind him and walked outside. The barking was explosive, now, and continuous.

He hesitated, standing on the dry grass. He and his neighbor weren't friends. The way to go to his house in the middle of the night would be to go round to the front of the house, down his own front walk, along the short stretch of sidewalk, and in at next-door's front walk. But…well, he had nothing on but a raincoat. He over-lapped it, knotted the belt and cut through his own back yard. He stepped through the bushy boundary between the two properties and walked toward the sound as though he were following a line drawn for him.

He was right. The dogs were tied up. They were on short ropes, the other ends of the tethers tied around a big old maple tree. They were leaping frantically toward him, their front feet off the ground as their collars hauled them back from each lunge. He walked past them. He wasn't scared of dogs. He knew dogs. He could handle dogs. These ones were sure crazy, though, he thought.

He walked across the front porch, slapping the boards with his overlarge boots, and knocked on the door. Nobody heard, of course. His knock was like a finger snap against the constant back-ground of noise. Now that he was up here, he could see how it was they could stand the noise of the dogs. A television inside was on at a terrific volume. The boom of declamatory voices crashed with waves of laughter not just through the closed door but, it seemed, from every surface of the frame house. They were probably the only people in the county who couldn't hear their dogs. He knocked more, and harder. He rang the doorbell over and over, although he had an idea from the look of it that the doorbell didn't work. He waited. Nothing. He rang again, knocked again. The dogs were ecstatic with excitement, but there was no response from indoors. He walked to the big window and looked in. The man—what was his name? Shameful not to know your neighbors. In the old house they'd known everybody in the neighborhood—the man was asleep, dead to the world on the sofa, his head back on the cush-ions, his legs splayed out before him. In his hand was a beer can. Or some kind of a can. Could have been Pepsi. All the lights were on. He knocked on the window, but he couldn't make much noise on the glass unless he hit it hard enough to break it, so he went back to the door. He wasn't going to go back without getting this done. For sure.

He was just about to walk around and try the back door—not that he thought he'd have any better luck there—when he saw a child on the stairs. A boy about Peter's age—a little older, maybe—creased and rumpled all over: hair, pajamas, even his cheek, with the imprint of the wrinkles of his pillowcase on it. The little boy opened the door (why hadn't he been taught never to open the door without knowing who was on the other side?) and gazed up at Jeff.

"Hey," said Jeff. The child was blinking in the light. "Can I talk to your dad?"

The boy nodded and walked into the living room. Jeff stayed at the door, watching. Could his mother still be asleep? Maybe there wasn't a mother. Poor kid. The boy pulled on the man's arm, without any effect that Jeff could see. Except that his head bobbed over onto his shoulder a little more. Dear Christ, I hope he's not dead! But, with no seeming anxiety or sense of hurry, the child kept pulling and pushing and finally the man opened his eyes and looked first at the TV, then at his son. There was no hearing what the boy said, but the man nodded and pushed himself heavily off the couch. He was a big man when he stood up, the belly Jeff had noticed while he was sleeping distributed somehow over a long torso. Jeff was surprised to see him bend over and kiss the top of his boy's head. He steered the child toward the stairs and patted his seat to send him on his way. The boy started carefully to climb the stairs without looking again at his father or at Jeff.

The man proceeded to the door and said, "Hey."

"Hey. I just came over to see if you were okay. I'm sure glad to see you are."

The man looked at him steadily. "Yeah?" he said finally.

"Well, I heard your dogs was barkin' so long, I thought there must be somethin' the matter, so I came over to see." There was a pause. "Dogs don't usually keep it up so long." Jeff smiled.

The man nodded. "No," he said, "there ain't nothin' the matter. Don't worry about the dogs. I'll see to 'em."

"Well, that's fine. I'll be on my way, then."

The man nodded again. "Thank you for callin'," he said.

"Well..." Jeff hesitated, "neighbors..."

"Sure thing."

"Goodnight then."

"You too," the man said.

As Jeff walked across the yard toward his own house, the note of the dogs' racket altered. He looked back and saw that their master had put them both on one leash and was dragging the creatures toward the house. The next time he looked, he was pushing them through the front door. Standing amongst their common forsythia and sweetbud bushes he could hear the creatures still baying or howling or whatever it was they did, but muffled. He realized that they were going to go on barking all night inside the house. He shook his head and laughed out loud. A nice guy, his next door neighbor. He was sorry he hadn't asked his name, glad he had got through it without making an enemy of him. Who knew how he could sleep. Clear conscience, maybe.

When he got back, Laurel was awake, standing in the back doorway looking for him. "I didn't have any idea in this world where you'd gone," she said. She watched as he kicked off the boots in the entryway.

He was surprised at her tone. She sounded...worried? More than worried. Edgy. As though she'd been through something. "Well, Laurel," he put his arm around her shoulders, "You knew I hadn't gone far."

"No, I didn't! I didn't!" No doubting now the quality of her voice. Reproachful. Just this side of angry. Scared, even. "You should 'a told me you was goin' out!"

"Well, I wasn't gonna wake you up just for that. Besides," he smiled, "you could 'a guessed. Listen." They were silent for a moment and then he turned to her. "What d'you hear?"

"Nothin'. I can't hear a thing."

"That's just right! I was out shuttin' those dogs up."

He had caught her attention. She looked at him, turning in his light encirclement. "Jeff, what did you do? You didn't...hurt them, did you?"

He took her hand and she moved with him toward their room. "Lord, woman! No, I didn't. What do you think I am? I don't go round shootin' other people's dogs in the middle of the night."

"Well...I didn't say shooting, only...what did you do?"

"I talked to the man. Mister dog-man."

"Franklin. Their name's Franklin."

"How did you know that? I didn't know his name."

"His wife brings the littlest one to Day Care."

"At the church?"

She nodded.

"I never seen them at church."

"They don't go to our church. I'm not sure if they go to church.

That child didn't know any Bible stories when he first came. Not even Noah's Ark. Myra had to teach him a little grace to say before juice and cookies when it was his turn."

"I didn't think he'd got a wife. The state of that place."

"She's a nice woman, Jeff. Judge not that ye be not judged."

"That's the truth," he said. Then he added, "I just can't believe, Laurie, that I'm standin' here in the middle of the night in a dirty raincoat talkin' about next door's religion."

He waited for her to smile, but she frowned. "You can't tell what will happen," she said. "A little child shall lead them. Who knows but what that baby brings home from Day Care will be the saving of them all."

He took the coat off and dropped it over the back of the bedroom chair.

"You're naked," she said.

"Well, I can't deny it, Laurel, but I used to have a raincoat on."

"She didn't reply. She watched him as he moved toward the bed.

"Well, Laurel…" he said, "I am in my own bedroom in the middle of the night." He got himself under the sheet, oddly embarrassed.

He relaxed into his pillow. "Are you okay?" he asked. You seem kind of…are you upset?"

She shook her head. "Just glad to have you back," she said. "Safe and sound." Then she leaned over him and kissed him. First tenderly, lips to closed lips, then deeply, breathlessly, and her cool fingers slipped down over his warm skin. Her night-scented hair hung over his face. He was aroused and bewildered. "Laurel," he said, "what's come over you?"

She laughed into his mouth, into the hollow of his neck, into his chest. "Nothin'," she said, "I'm just glad you're here. I just thought I'd kiss you with the kisses of my mouth, while I've got the chance. If you don't mind."

"How crazy d'you think I am, woman?" and he drew her into his embrace.

When she finally looked again at the clock, she said, "You're gonna have to sleep fast. You've only got three hours before Alan's gonna be in here jumpin' on you."

"Runs in the family," he said, smiling into the dark.

They lay silent. Finally, ready to sink into sleep, he said, "Why were you so worried anyway, Laurie? You'd been cryin'."

"Never mind," she said. "It all turned out all right. I'll tell you in the morning. Go to sleep."

In the morning they shut the windows against the growing heat, got the children dressed, had their breakfast together and began another day. There wasn't time to talk about the events of their disturbed night.

†

The next Sunday they all went to his sister's place for dinner. Jeff told them about the dogs and what Tod, his sister's husband, called his "midnight ramble." Everybody laughed and Tod said, "You are one hell of a diplomat!" Laurel looked briefly toward her children, but they were playing on the stairs, too far away to hear their uncle's careless language.

"Well," she began, "while he was out bein' a diplomat, I woke up in an empty bed. Nobody there. 'I sought him and I found him not.' Not a sound to be heard."

"Well, there was your clue," said Jeff.

"There was not a soul to be seen," she resumed, "and I called out. 'Jeff!' I said, 'Where are you?' and there wasn't a word of an answer. So I got up out of bed and went to hunt for him. There wasn't a light on in the bathroom, but I knocked on the door anyway, and then I went in, and it was dark, and he wasn't there. And he wasn't in the kitchen gettin' a drink, and he wasn't in the livin' room, and he wasn't down the cellar, and he wasn't anyplace. So I went back into our room and looked again. There was his pajamas all in the bed, and his shoes and his slippers both sittin' on the rug. And it was so quiet. And there wasn't any moon. And I thought, Oh, my dear Lord Jesus, it's come. The Rapture has come and Jeff has been caught up. And I got down on my knees on the rug and I said, 'Jesus Christ, my Lord and Savior, come back for me.' But I knew it couldn't be. I knew I'd been left behind to endure the Tribulations by myself. Oh, I can't tell you how lost I felt in that time!"

"Laurel!" said Jeff, "Oh, my Laurie." He got up from the table and moved toward her, but she motioned him away and went on.

"I'd thought I was saved, but in that hour I thought of all the times I'd doubted my salvation, and all the times I'd said the words of a prayer while my mind wasn't there, and I thought how easy it was to think you're hearin' the voice of the Lord when really it's the deceitful urgings of the devil that you're listenin' to. Like Eve in the garden. And Jeff never talks about it like I do, and I thought, well, that's because I'm like the scribes and the Pharisees, prayin' for outward show. I always knew he was a good man. I always knew he was a saved man."

The others watched her, silenced by the flow of her passionate telling. Her eyes were hot and bright, but she did not cry.

"And then," she went on, "I thought of my children. I thought to go and look into their rooms, even though I knew they would be gone, in their innocence.

"I went into Peter's room and my heart just about stopped when I saw him layin' there. The first thing I thought was we never should 'a let him be baptized at Easter. He was awful young, but it seemed like he understood, and he wanted to accept Jesus into his life and I thought it was a security for him, in his growin' up in the world children have to be in in these times. But bein' baptized made him the same as a grown man in the eyes of the Lord, and he was responsible for his own sins. No..." she interrupted herself, as though afraid one of the others would interrupt her first. "I know it's not exactly that way. I'm just sayin' how it looked to me in that terrible midnight hour. And I thought he had been left behind with me to face war and pestilence, famine and death. I could 'a screamed like a panther then and there, but you know...he just looked so peaceful and so...so *good* layin' there, I wanted to leave him in peace as long as I could. So I shut the door and I went next door and went into Alan's room and do you know, I put the light on, that's how sure I was he wouldn't be there. But there he was. His legs all splayed out all over the place like he does. And he turned his head around to get his eyes away from the light. And that's when I knew that it wasn't the Rapture after all, because my innocent baby would never a been left.

"So I kissed him and pulled the sheet up over him where he'd kicked it off, and I turned off the light and went out into the other room to wait for Jeff to come home. And I thanked God for givin' me a little more time to perfect my salvation. And I still do thank Him."

No one spoke. Finally Jeff said, "Laurel, you...Laurel, your price is above rubies," and Tod said, "Well, that is the dam—the durndest thing I ever heard." Nancy did not speak.

"I take it as a warnin' not to slumber and sleep," said Laurel. "God sure got my attention on that night." She laughed a little, then sobered. "One day it won't be a mistake. It's to come one day soon. I take it as a warnin'."

Jack at the Mercy Seat

What various hindrances we meet
In coming to the Mercy Seat
Yet who that knows the worth of prayer
But wishes to be often there
—W. Cowper and Dr. L. Mason, "The Mercy Seat"

Jack was born in 1926, just too late for the fizz and frivolity of the Roaring Twenties. Not that there was much fizz, frivolity, or roaring in High Ridge, North Carolina. But the tannery was doing good business and reliably hiring the fourteen year olds who came out of school unqualified to do anything else. And the mills were working, turning out stockings (full fashioned, with seams) and tricot and bolts of printed dress cottons and upholstery damasks and artificial silk. The furniture factories kept men and women busy making and finishing suites of maple, beech, and oak, which were shipped north to where people could afford to buy them. Jack was born just in time for the Great Depression. His dad was laid off the day before Jack's fourth birthday.

The family was poor when he was little, but Jack was dearly loved, well appreciated, generously praised. He was the youngest of three children—five years younger than his brother and seven years younger than his sister. The years between them were so many that the older children, well accustomed to competing with one another, were not inclined to compete with Jack. Rather, they petted him, carried him (Sharon on her hip, the way her mother did, Dick on his back, with Jack's arms tightened in a strangle-tight grip round his neck), and vied with one another for his preference. Only sometimes they had more important things to do. They were in school; they had friends. Dick and Sharon were Jack's only friends, but they were the only ones he needed.

When he was six, and had just started school, he noticed for the first time how much younger he was than his brother and sister. His mother told him that was because he was a gift from God. He was God's surprise present to her and his father, just like Isaac was for Sarah and Abraham when she thought she was too old to have any children. Sharon, who was fourteen and who knew everything, said, "You know what that really means? It means you were a mistake." Jack did not doubt that Sharon was telling him the truth, but he couldn't work out what she meant. And Sharon wouldn't say anything more. In fact, Sharon didn't know as much about babies as she pretended, not as much as her friends seemed to know. She kind of wished she'd never brought it up, now. She hadn't expected little Jack to keep talking about it. "You're too little to understand," she told him. "Just forget it." But how could a person be a mistake? His daddy said, "Now that was a mistake," sometimes, trying to teach Jack about hammering and sawing when a nail went in crooked or the saw blade skittered off its mark, "That was a mistake. We better do it over again." How could you do a person over again if he was a mistake? Not with nails. Was that understanding something that waited in his future, like the long division Daddy darkly talked about?

He had to ask his mother, finally. She said, "I'll have something to say to little miss know all." For the first time it occurred to him that Sharon and not he was in the wrong, and that was a relief. "Don't you think another thing about it," Grace told him. "Do you think God makes mistakes?" He shook his head, but the story of Noah and the flood sat uneasily in his memory, when God said He was sorry he'd ever made Man in the first place. "You're part of God's own plan. We can't even imagine what God has for you to do, but we know it's something. And," she went on, "you're my own dear boy." He was reassured about being his mother's own dear boy but a bit apprehensive about having something to do for God.

By then he wasn't seeing much of his dad, who couldn't find a job, though he worked all the time. There was still some work in High Ridge, and after a few years, F. D. Roosevelt's New Deal kicked in and the federal government started hiring. The local people made fun of the WPA workers, leaning on their shovels, doing work that didn't need doing, and of the younger ones, who would have been in the tannery in good days, out messing around in the woods for the Civilian Conservation Corps. They shook their heads at the foolishness of those politicians in Washington, but in the worst months, government wages were the only wages coming into some houses. Richard wouldn't have anything to do with federal handouts. He disdained them. He and Grace argued about it. They argued after Jack's bedtime in an attempt to keep the fights from him; the older children were made anxious by the raised voices, the slamming doors, but Jack rarely woke.

Their diet, which had always been simple, became increasingly limited but that didn't hurt as much as wearing tight shoes. "We'll get you a new pair a ways further down in the fall," Grace said. 1934 was the first year they didn't have new shoes to start the school year in. The children got new shoes for Christmas that year.

Richard said he wouldn't beg from that load of bandits in Washington. But he begged—he wouldn't have put it that way—short spells of work from whoever was hiring. He did things he would never have imagined himself doing. For a week, to cover somebody's sick leave, he collected buckets of shit from outdoor toilets. Then the regular man came back and that job was gone too, and the pick-up truck that went with it. Richard owned a truck himself, but he had trouble buying gas for it. He said that he'd do anything legal, with the private addition that it wouldn't have to be very legal. But in fact, the most menial jobs were the first to go. All the boys straight out of school went for them, and so did the skilled unemployed. Richard was unlucky that his job, mending and maintaining the glossy modern looms, had been shared between two men and when the tightening up came, the factory only needed one and it was the other one. He was senior; Richard couldn't complain. He spent a lot of time in the garden, as other men did. There wasn't much to come out of it in the wintertime—cabbages for a while, and brussels sprouts, which didn't wilt so bad in the hard frost. He sometimes retrieved turnips that had been missed, and even shriveled they added some heat to a stew. As the winter deepened, the ground became almost impossible to work, but still he spent hours outdoors grinding a fork into frozen clods. When he came in, his hands were stiff and red, almost without feeling. Grace's heart was wrung by his poor hands. She would take them in hers and hold them against her skin, under her clothes, to warm them.

Richard wouldn't put up with disobedience or what they called "sass." His children knew he loved them, but it wasn't like the way their mother loved them. They understood the love and the fear of God as exaggerations of the way they felt about their father. Richard had always said "a wallop learns a child the difference between right and wrong," and they didn't expect to get away without one if they transgressed. Grace threatened them with their father more often than she reported them to him. That was one of the things they loved her for. When Sharon was in her teens, she was too old to be spanked. You couldn't pull a girl over your knee when she was nearly a woman. Even though you could say, "Don't think you're too old for a whuppin'!" she was. And Jack was too small. He had swift smacks on his bottom, through his trousers and his underpants, or sharp blows to his hands. "Don't touch!" Richard knew he didn't like hurting his children. He did it for their own good. Sometimes, he said, you just have to give them a whuppin'. He didn't beat them. Not like some fathers. He loved his children. They depended on him. They were smaller than he was.

It was only worry over money and the hard times stretching on. It was the hard cold earth, uneven from digging and hard to walk on. It was not being able to sleep, however tired he was. It was having waited so long to sign up that the WPA gang was full. Jack had never seen a beating like the one his father gave Dick. He had never imagined it.

"Please, please, please!" he screamed. He grabbed his father's furious arm with both his small hands, trying to interrupt the horrible, rhythmic pump-action of the machine that the man seemed to have become. There was blood on Dick's thin legs, enough to gather in little pools in the hollows behind his knees, to drip, to spread onto his trousers. The father's blows went on. It was as though there would never be an end to them. And Jack's voice went on. "Please, please, please!" until he was breathless and hoarse.

Their mother came. She had walked from town and was pink with hurrying in the cold. She entered the kitchen running, following Jack's voice and the other sounds that came from there. Her purse, her bag of shopping, fell away from her as she came. Jack knew that she was there, but he seemed to have caught whatever his father had; he could not stop his hands rising and falling with his father's arms; he could not stop crying, "please, please, please!" Then her hands were on Jack's hands, on Richard's arm, on Dickie's bleeding thighs, and it stopped. She put her arms around Dick and pulled him toward her. Richard straightened himself and looked at her, frowning slightly, blinking. Dick began to cry, his head muffled in his mother's coat collar. Richard said, "It looks a lot worse than it is," and he turned and walked out of the room.

Jack was not to remember what happened next. Mother must have washed Dick's bottom and legs. She must have wrapped them up in clean rags, the way she did when he scraped himself falling off his bike. She must have held him while he cried. Perhaps she had told Jack to go out of the room, but what would have been the use of that? Years later, when Grace told the story, she said, "He tore my baby up with a rosebush! He tore into him with a thorned switch!" But Jack couldn't remember that. When he imagined it, he pictured blood standing on roses like dew. But there wouldn't have been roses. It was winter.

That spring, Richard got a part time job in the store alongside the Texaco station. He did the graveyard shift, so he went out straight after supper and got back to drink strong coffee at breakfast time. Sometimes he had funny stories about the people who came in to the store while he was there. There was a woman who bought root beer for her dog. She always borrowed a bucket and poured two cans into it and then talked to Dad while the dog lapped up the drink, blinking as the bubbles came up. "She seems like she's in her right mind, except for that." And once he came home with a scary story. A young man came in the store with a shotgun, "he pointed it right at my head," and told him to hand over all the money in the cash register. "What did you do?" "Well, hell, I would ha' give it to him. There weren't but a few dollars there. Old man Martin always empties it out and takes it with him at seven when the shift changes. But I never had to…" He paused while the children and Grace watched his face, "'cause those Goudge boys came in, tanked up like always, makin' so much noise he got spooked and run off." He laughed, and they all did, relieved and excited. His wife would fry him a plateful of potatoes and when he had eaten them, he would take his boots and pants off and slide himself into the bed Grace had left, the covers tucked in carefully to preserve her warmth until he came back.

That spring, Dick said that he wanted to be baptized.

He was nearly twelve, not too young, and his mother had been watching him carefully for signs of the conviction of sin. She meant to establish beyond doubt that it was not the drama of the day that attracted him, or the seal on his adult status. This was a perilous time for the life of his spirit. When she first asked him why he wanted to be baptized, he said, "Because I love Jesus." Jack, watching, saw that his mother did not smile, as he expected, but frowned.

"Dickie," (Dickie was a baby name that he had outgrown for normal use) "everybody loves Jesus, because Jesus is Love. But that's not the same thing as bein' saved."

"Yes, but I am saved, I know."

She went on. "Love is just a feeling. Anybody can have feelings. No, if you're baptized, you give yourself to the Lord forever. It's like this: when you're older, you'll find out about human love. You'll find some girl you think you love just because you have feelings for her."

"Mama, don't."

"And that might happen four or five times. But all those little girls. You might want to hug and kiss and do all those carnal things…"

"I won't either."

"But you won't really love one until you're ready to marry her. Do you know what you say when you get married?"

Dick was looking straight at the floor between his shoes. He didn't answer.

"I know!" said Jack. Dick had forgotten he was there. The older boy sighed ostentatiously and shifted his gaze from the floor to the wall. "You say for-staking-all-the-others and keep…and keep…"

"Well, now that's not quite right," Mama said. This time she was smiling, so Jack knew that what he had said was better than what Dick had said, even if it wasn't quite right. "But you've struck on the right word. It's 'forsaking.' Now Dick, what does that mean?"

"It means you have to give up… does he have to be here?"

"He needs to learn, too." But she told Jack to go play outdoors and he didn't much mind. He had had about enough.

But Dick said the right thing eventually, Jack knew, because he was allowed to be baptized.

On the day, Dick wore the nearest thing to a suit that his mother could contrive—a jacket of his father's with its sleeves shortened and a pair of trousers almost the same color blue, a shirt that was pure white and starched to a reflective shine. Jack wondered why his mother had taken so much trouble, because Dick changed out of it into a sort of nightshirt before he went up to be dunked. He had to go right under, head and all. The preacher held him down while he prayed. It was only for as long as it takes to say, "Bless thy servant Richard Andrew and sanctify him to your use," but Jack was sure he would drown. "Will he go straight to heaven if he drowns?"

"Shh."

Afterward, when Dick was back in his best clothes, Jack asked him if he still loved Jesus. "Of course," Dick said. "Only it isn't about love. It's about sin."

†

When it was Jack's turn to be baptized, it was 1936 and it looked like times were never going to get any better. He was eleven and Dick was sixteen, nearly seventeen. He remembered to say about sin when he and the preacher had their talk. He said he wanted to take Jesus as his personal savior because Jesus's blood would wash away his sin. He climbed up wooden stairs behind sky blue curtains that framed the baptismal pool. The pool was a zinc-lined tank that stood on a platform. The platform was high on stilts. Jack had seen the stairs and the tank and the platform before; his friends were mostly getting baptized. He didn't expect it to be like heaven…but the wooden steps were as ordinary as back porch steps and even the curtains were just like anybody's window curtains. Dick had told him that he would feel lifted up as he stepped into the water. He said, "Don't worry if your ears ring; that's just the sound of heaven singing all around you." He looked out at the congregation who were just eight steps below him but seemed far away, and there were his mother and father, sitting with Sharon and Dick between them, and between Sharon and Dick was the empty place where he would sit to listen to the sermon and sing the closing hymn after he was baptized. After he was baptized, he knew, everything would be different.

The congregation was singing, but through the water in his ears, he did not hear heaven.

As he had followed Dick into the acceptance of Christ, so Jack followed him into the army. Dick had joined in 1939 because it was the best job he could find. He would have his board and lodging, he argued to his mother, and his on-duty clothes, so he would have to spend almost none of his pay, which was already a lot better than the tannery paid, even if the tannery was taking on, and it wasn't. He could send money home. Richard said they could do without the money. Grace said things were picking up. If he remained patient for a little longer, she was sure that a real good job would come up. He was old enough to sign up without their permission, but he probably would not have gone without their blessing. "They'll learn him a trade," Grace said to his father. They were both sure that the war threatening in Europe wouldn't come to anything. Or even if it did, that America wouldn't join in. Richard, who had been out of the United States twice, once to Mexico when he was hoboing around in his teens and once to France in 1917, did say, "Well, we did the last time," but really they expected Dick to be a peacetime soldier. Grace even thought that army life might be good for him. It might settle him down. He hadn't been led into bad ways, but she sometimes thought that he had bad companions and that day after day without a job, with nothing to do but kill time, was not wholesome for him. He was bored with things. He might be looking at the wrong kind of women.

Dick was overseas even before Pearl Harbor, and from then on they were afraid all the time.

Jack joined up as soon as he could. He didn't wait to be drafted. He was sent to Georgia, then to San Francisco for just long enough to get on a ship to the Philippines. The sailors told them that ships got blown up on this route after three round trip and this was their fourth. Jack knew it was a joke by the way they laughed, but he was afraid of what might be pursuing him, waiting for him under the sea.

His outfit landed on Leyte at the beginning of December. He learned that the 24th Infantry had taken it back from the Japs in the fall. They had classes every morning. Luzon was the biggest island of the group. Manila was the capital and it was on Luzon. The Japs still had that one and the infantry was going to have to take it back sometime soon. The 6th Army. Take the big island and the Bataan Peninsula and Corrigidor. He'd still been a kid when the Japanese had taken over Bataan. His new buddies told him about the Bataan Death March. Maybe they weren't telling the folks back home what it was like, or maybe he just hadn't been paying attention. He had really only cared about where Dick was and Dick was not in the Philippines. They didn't cover the death march in the classes, but he heard all the stories about what the Japs did to the men they captured. They hated prisoners, Jack heard, for not dying.

So up north was the big island where the big battle was going to be and down here in the south was this bunch of little islands. It was calm here. He learned a few words of Spanish. The Filipinos all talked Spanish. That was a surprise. And it was a surprise that they were all Catholics. One afternoon he and some of his buddies walked out to an old Catholic church. "Many hundreds years old," the Flip boy told them. "It looks like it," Jack said. He sent a photograph home with his next letter. "They don't take care of their churches like we do," he wrote. When he read it over before he put it into the envelope, he added, "I guess they have a hard time doing repairs with the war going on." He sent a picture of some girls, too, and some grinning kids. The girls liked the GI's; they were always around the camp. They weren't as pretty as the girls at home; they were too dark and their faces were kind of flat. But their eyes were beautiful, like black water in leaf-shaped pools. They were supposed to wear blouses when they were in the camp, but they didn't cover their breasts in their villages or in the fields. They didn't seem to think anything of it. The old men, who had been there a while, said that you get used to it, but Jack never did. He had never seen a woman's breasts before.

Back home he had a girlfriend, Lucille, whose breasts he had touched, but only through her sweater. He carried her picture with him and wrote to her every week. When he came home after his basic training, before he shipped out, she promised to wait for him. They put "Don't Sit Under the Apple Tree (With Anyone Else But Me)" on the jukebox and kissed each other. She dropped tears onto his rough wool collar.

They invaded Mindoro in the middle of December, just ten days before Christmas. He had his mother's card with him. It had glittery snow on it that fell off. He found the little flakes of white glitter embedded in his khaki pocket even after it had been in the laundry. As Jack waded ashore he could see parachutes swinging downward through gentle air, white as mushrooms.

He thanked God he had arrived safely. Maybe too soon for thanksgiving, before the battle began, but it was on board ship that he had felt in danger. The ship he was on was a troop carrier, but all around him were warships, ready to be attacked. The Japs were crazy. Something about the war had driven them insane, or maybe they had always been insane and that was why they started the war. They were deliberately crashing their planes into ships. It had started during the Battle of Leyte Gulf in October, and at first the Americans and the Filipinos thought it was an accident. But they were doing it on purpose. Not just taking a risk. They weren't daredevils, like the boys who dived down so low to drop their bombs that they were sometimes swallowed up in the explosions before they could get away. They never had any intention of getting away. They were making themselves into bombs. Just a few days ago one of them had crashed into the *Nashville* and killed 130 men. And himself, of course. Jack had been to Nashville once. He and Dick had gone to see the Grand Ole Opry together and had gone out drinking beer in bars. It really felt like being brothers then. Funny, he thought, that they should call a battle cruiser Nashville.

This was a beautiful place. The beach was white and narrow and you could see where the land started to rise, covered in green. You could see the mountains, their tops lost in cloud, farther off. "I'd rather be in New Jersey!" Big Jack said, and everybody laughed. In their induction classes they'd been told that Mindoro was half the size of New Jersey.

He could have forgotten that he was invading the island, the air was so warm, so softly damp, so full of the smell of earth and grass. He reacted without thinking when the Jap soldier appeared. Jack shot, then looked around for the others. But the one he shot was the only one. There was no one else between the trees. He heard someone say, "Hell, yes!" and he took in a quick breath. It took him a second to recognize a friend voice. Then it was quiet; some kind of bird was calling with a repetitive, metallic cry. He had the sense that he and the rest of the men were tiptoeing in their big boots. They had all stopped, like his shot had stopped everything, but now they were moving forward in a wavy line, hesitating, then stepping, as though they were dancing.

He came to the place where the Jap he had brought down lay. The man's forage cap had fallen off and his black hair—longer, Jack thought, than he would have got away with in his army—fell toward the ground. He looked at his face, thought that yellow wasn't exactly the right word for the color of it and lifted his left foot to step over the man's outflung arm. As he looked down, the fingers clenched. He jumped back, afraid now as he had not had time to be afraid before. The ground was soaking up the blood as fast as it came out. He watched the brown earth turn black in a widening arc, like a halo around the head. The long black hair was turning sticky as he watched. Big Jack was next to him and he caught his shoulder. "What's the matter with you?" he said.

"He's alive."

Big Jack looked across at the man who should have been a corpse. "Not for long," he said.

Somebody further down the line laughed.

The Jap's head was moving back and forth. There was no sound, but his mouth made the shape of a scream. Jack saw what was wrong. His shot had been too low to kill him. "Sorry," he said, and he shot him again, this time aiming at his chest.

"What'd you do that for? He wasn't gonna get up and follow us."

"My daddy always said to kill a wounded animal," Jack said.

"Hell, he meant a stag. This was just a Jap."

They walked fearfully after that, looking out for men hiding behind trees, in pits, crouched in bushes. Men who would have been alerted by Jack's two shots. But they saw no one. Jack was the only one to kill an enemy. Later one of his buddies reminded him that he should have taken the Jap's rifle. If he didn't want to keep it for a souvenir, he could have traded it. He was entitled. "I sure don't want it enough to go back for it," Jack said.

The landing was accomplished, Lucille and his parents read in the papers, "against relatively light opposition."

There wasn't any real fighting after the first day. The occasional straggler like Jack's Jap. It looked like the Japs didn't want the island any more than the Americans did. The only reason for being on Mindoro was to get to Luzon. They were really there to support the engineers who were building airfields, so the work became familiar. It was just laboring.

"We had a real good Christmas dinner," Jack wrote to Grace, "but I sure was homesick for your cooking." To Lucille he wrote, "I miss you something awful. Next Christmas we'll be in our own little place, what do you say?" To his father, "I'm working so hard I might as well have stayed in High Ridge!"

"Tomorrow we're heading off for Luzon." It was New Year's Eve. All the men cheered, Jack with them. Luzon was the whole point. Once they took Luzon they would have won. This part of the war, anyway. It was going to be a big fleet; there would be naval and air bombardment before the landings. The name of each ship with its tonnage and weaponry was read out, and at each name, they all cheered. Even as Jack cheered he felt sick fear. He looked around at the others and he could see that none of them was afraid. "You bastards will be on the *USS Colorado!*" The biggest cheer of all.

They would sleep their last night in barracks and board the *Colorado* before dawn. Jack rolled his clothes up and stowed them in his bag. Then he went for a walk. They were at liberty until chow time. He made for a ruined chapel he'd seen in amongst the trees a few miles down the track. There used to be a school, too, he'd been told, but the climate on the island was unhealthy. There was malaria, and sicknesses you'd never even heard of. The mountains trapped the clouds and it rained almost every day. When it wasn't raining the air was thick with damp. Even when it wasn't hot you were covered with sweat within a few minutes of any kind of exercise. It was a hell of a climate to build airfields in. As he walked, he could feel the sun sullenly burning through layers of blanketing cloud.

The chapel was roofless and the walls had almost been replaced by climbing vines and creepers. He walked over broken tiles toward a stone altar. At first he thought it had been decorated, but as he got closer he saw that some kind of white-flowering creeper had covered it like a cloth. Above it, where the green growth was less luxuriant, he saw what might have been the shadow of a cross on the pitted stone wall. Maybe where the cross used to be. The crucifix. He reminded himself that it would have been a Catholic church. He guessed the church furniture would have been moved out when the people left it. Long ago, probably, even before the Japanese came, if it was so unhealthy here. He knelt down and tried to pray, but nothing came. He didn't know what to ask for. He wanted to live through the invasion of Luzon, but he didn't see why he should. There were going to be thousands of men on dozens of ships. Some of them were going to die. What difference did it make to God which ones? He thought of the day he was baptized, of the preacher's hand flat on his head, of Dick's hand on his shoulder.

"God," he said. "God, I'm just sorry for ever'thing I've done wrong." He opened his eyes and looked into those of the wide trumpet shaped flowers before him. "I don't know," he said, "I don't know." He closed his eyes again and said, "In the name of thy son, Jesus Christ, Amen." He stayed there a while longer, not thinking anything, feeling the emptiness of the building that used to be a church, that used to be a building. Then he got up, slowly like an old man, feeling his calves ache, and walked back to camp.

That night Jack wondered if he was the only one who was shouting "Happy New Year" just so he wouldn't be the only one not to. There was beer but not enough to get drunk on, and they were keeping the Filipinos away, so there was no local liquor. They tried to be merry. Somebody shouted, "Come on, boys, this is your last chance to raise hell!" but there was a silence afterward and a feeling of embarrassment. "Shit, I just meant before the invasion." But they did not revive. The sergeant came in and said they should go to bed. "I wouldn't order you to retire on New Year's Eve," he said, sounding almost gentle, "but you're not going to have much sack time anyhow." Jack was relieved. It was an effort to stay up until midnight. Last year, he hadn't gone to bed at all, but stomped onto the front porch at sunup, laughing at the sight of his mother's face, trying to reflect fury and relief at the same time, just like after all the other scrapes he'd been in over the years. You could tell she wanted to hit him and hug him both and couldn't decide which to do first. She'd brought him in and made him drink coffee and then he went out and threw up in the yard. He thought back on it now with fondness. He wished his mother could get mad at him now. He wished nothing worse was going to happen to him than vomiting behind the bushes.

Some of the boys were still singing when he got into his bunk (he recognized Redwing, the dirty version), but it didn't bother him. It sounded cheerful through the end wall. When he was a kid, he had only been allowed to say his prayers in bed if he was sick, but in barracks he always did. "Now I lay me down to sleep," he began, "I pray the Lord my soul to keep; if I should die before I wake I pray the Lord my soul to take, amen." He knew grown-up prayers, but right now he couldn't call any to mind. "Bless Mother and Father and Dick and Sharon and…" he went on with the old childish list, adding a few he hadn't included for a while; Aunt Ruth who lived out west and Jacob, who used to be his friend at school. Jacob was the best friend he had in those days, but he hadn't had any really good friends. Dick was his best friend. He started working his way through his outfit. God bless Frank and Big Jack. God bless… When he woke up, the singing had stopped. The sky was black, with a pale shadow where the last sliver of moon hung behind clouds. He had fallen asleep during his prayers. "Amen," he said. He wondered how long it was until morning. He felt as though he had slept all he was going to. He looked wide-eyed from the dark sky into the dark room. A different quality of dark and nothing to be seen. He shut his eyes, retreating to the darkness he carried with him behind his eyelids. His mother's face was there again. Perhaps he had been dreaming about her, but he couldn't remember now. Only her face, angry and loving at the same time.

In the morning they were all laughing, shouting, making too much noise. A little redheaded man called Art said, "Hey, you know what day the Flips call this? The Feast of Three Kings!"

"You're just pig ignorant," said one of the guys from New York. "That's not today, it's next…" he paused for a second, calculating, "Saturday. The sixth. It's the day the kings came with gifts. Epiphany." Jack had already worked out they were Catholics. Something about the way they talked. Something about the way they stuck together.

"Well, you sure as hell know a lot of shit!" This came from among the cluster at the door, amongst the heaving of kit bags, the shoving forward. The New York guy shrugged and finished rolling up his

mattress, then he, too, moved toward the door. They were all passing through, and Jack felt he had missed an opportunity to speak
up for Jesus. He should have said something about "hell" and "shit"
so close to Christ's manger. But now it was too late.

†

Onboard the ship, in the dark afternoon, he watched silently
while one of the old men lit a cigarette. They were sitting on the
deck with their backs against a bulkhead, not quite listening to
the steady thrum of the ship moving ahead, not quite seeing the
glimpses of olive land that sometimes colored the gray air at a distance, and then faded into gray again.

The other man said, through the smoke that filled his mouth,
"You know about this ship, don't you?"

Jack shook his head, nervous, wanting to hear and wanting not
to hear the story that was impending.

"Blown all to hell last November."

"What do you mean?" Maybe this character was crazy. Maybe he
thought they were all ghosts already, on a ship that had been blown
to hell. Jack was cold in his stomach. Had he ever seen this man
before? Where had he come from?

"Kamikazes," he said.

"Kamikazes."

"Hell, yes! Those crazy bastards fly out from Tokyo and drive
straight into a ship."

"I know what they are."

But the man would not stop. He had lit a fresh cigarette and blew
his gray smoke into the gray air. He said, "They don't *carry* a bomb,
those fuckers *are* a fuckin' bomb!"

"I know."

"They can't even turn those planes around; they just go straight
ahead. Nose full of explosives, tank full of gas, pilot full of shit…"
He lifted his right arm suddenly and made a fast diving motion with
his hand across his body until it slammed onto the deck. "Wham!
Up she goes!"

Jack looked at the man's hand, flat on the deck. "I know what
they do," he made himself say.

"You ever seen it?" the man asked.

Jack shook his head. "You ever seen it? Were you here?"

The man laughed. His breath was full of smoke and his teeth
were long, like a horse's teeth, and yellowish. How old was he,
anyway, Jack wondered. Suddenly he seemed too old to be on this

operation. He did not move but he felt himself shrinking away from the presence beside him. He whispered, "Who are you?" but the man was still laughing. It sounded hollow, like the laughing man that stood outside the fairground in Washington D.C. The same ha ha ha, over and over. The laughing man was supposed to make you want to laugh too, but it never did.

Finally the laugh turned off and the man spoke. "Nineteen dead," he said, "seventy two wounded."

So he could have been one of the wounded.

"You should 'a seen the wounded washing the dead off 'em," he said. "Pieces of dead people no bigger than a dime. Red and black. Black ashes falling down out of the sky like they was snow. You couldn't tell what was Jap and what was American meat. You couldn't even tell what was meat and what was ship. Boy, you should 'a smelled it!"

The cigarette had died in his hand. He struck a match and relit it. The flame did not waver in the still air. Again he proffered the pack to Jack and again Jack shook his head. "Twenty-third of November," the man said, and shook his head. "Goddamn."

Jack looked away, out at the oil colored sea. The twenty-third of November—that would have been Thanksgiving. That must have been hell. Real hell. He turned back and the man was gone. Jack felt a deep, sick stab of fear. How could he be gone? They were side by side, almost touching. Even out of the corner of his eye he should have seen him get up. He would have heard him walk away, even the rustle of his clothes, the creak of his boots. He should have missed the animal warmth beside him. He put out a hand to touch the deck and felt no warmth there beyond the warmth of the shrouded sun.

Until dark he looked for the man. The ship was crawling with sailors and infantry and it seemed that everyone was moving. You could cover every inch and miss the man you were looking for because he was on the move, too. He ran into Big Jack and asked him if it was true that the *Colorado* had really been blown up.

"Hell, yes!"

"Why didn't they tell us?"

Big Jack shrugged. "'Fraid it'd spook us, I guess. They say it was the fastest repair and refit in the history of the US Navy. Let's hope it holds together, what d'you say?"

When night fell, he went into the cabin they had been assigned. They were supposed to sleep there until the first dawn. No one else was there yet. They had all congregated on deck, quiet and excited. There was no light, but there was liquor. Jack's mouth was burning with the sweet heat of bourbon. It was the night before the battle. He knelt down and started to say the twenty-third psalm. "Yea though I walk through the valley of the shadow of death I shall fear no evil for thou art with me." Suddenly he thought the man with the long teeth was kneeling next to him. He started, turned, searched the dim light for him, but there was nothing to see. There had been nothing this afternoon. "Thy rod and thy staff…" There was a laugh from somewhere. Drifting down from the deck. "Thy rod…spare the rod and spoil the child." No, not that; that was the wrong rod. He tried to concentrate on the precious blood of Jesus, shed for him, but he saw only Dick's blood, in little pools in the hollows behind his knees. He saw bloody pieces of men falling from the sky. They were falling and screaming, each bloody piece feeling a whole body's pain. He saw them fall into the fire on the deck, screaming with pain and then fly up again, "as the sparks fly upward," and then, swirling in the heat, the sharp grit, the dizzying, sickening fall back into the flames. He saw the diminishing tail of the kamikaze plane, growing lacy as it was consumed, sticking out of the hole in the deck. The hole was edged in yellow fire and its heart was black and filled with screaming. The deck, he saw, was as thin as paper and beneath it was hot black breath and the boiling sea that burned and burned with searing heat and no light and was not quenched.

The world, he saw, had just such a thin crust and tomorrow he would fall through it into hell. "Oh, sweet Jesus!" His baptism had been a sham. He had committed every sin. Women and girls had filled his foul imagination; he had even thought about pure Lucille that way. He had polluted himself. He had lied, he had stolen, he had taken the Lord's name in vain many times, he had caused his loving parents to grieve for him. While Dick was going closer to Jesus, he was going closer and closer to hell. He had forgotten God. Jesus God, there was whisky in his mouth this minute, with his immortal soul going to meet its judgment in just a few short hours. It would make God sick to look at him.

He had risen to look into the thin darkness for the devil he knew had been sent for him; now he sank down on his knees again and cried out, "Oh, Jesus, sweet Savior, save me! Oh, Jesus, save me by your precious blood!" Over and over again, through tears, he said Jesus's name. Finally, he heard something in his own voice

that wasn't horror, but longing. "It isn't about love," Dick had told
him, "It's about sin." He saw now: the sin first and then, oh then,
the love. There was a feeling he remembered from when he was
little, from when he'd done something bad and been punished,
and finally, when he'd been sad for long enough, Mama would put
her arms around him and say, "You're my good boy." It wasn't that,
but that was the nearest he could get to what he felt now. As though
Jesus were saying, "You're my good boy."

The crust of the world closed over again; the black boiling sea
was hidden. He stood up and wiped his face with his handkerchief,
blew his nose, pushed his fingers through his hair. He walked to the
door and looked at his watch in the red light of the gangway lamp.
It was 10:35, twenty two hours and thirty five minutes into the new,
sweet year of 1945.

Jack's unit took part in a small-scale operation that was designed
to deceive the Japanese about Allied intentions. They had little
effect on the main action. But of course they played their part. U.S.
and Filipino troops entered Manila on the third of February. Jack
was back home by Christmas.

†

Before he and Lucille were married, he told her that he had
been saved while he was out in the Pacific and she said, "Well, that's
fine." They had three children during the next five years. She sat
up in bed holding newborn Gracie and said, "Well, that's it. I'm
shutting up shop now."

He didn't try to rush her. He knew she was tired, and sore in her
woman's places. He could wait until it was time. But she never did
think it was time. He tried to convince her that when God made
husband and wife one flesh, he meant them to act like it, but she
was stubborn. "It's all I can do to look after these three," she said,
"without makin' any more." He promised he'd be careful. She just
laughed at that. He tried to raise his kids right, but she wasn't
a good disciplinarian. She let the kids run wild, he thought. He
asked his mom what she thought but she wouldn't say. He didn't
ask his dad, but he could tell the biggest one, Sandy, got on his
nerves, with her all the time talking and singing and running
around. Still, they were all right, him and Lucille. They got on, he
said, all right.

Then he found out that Lucille was cheating on him. He walked
right into his own house and found her sitting on the studio couch
with Earl Sawyer's arm around her. "I caught her red-handed," he

said. "I had 'em bang to rights, and she still had the nerve to tell me nothin' was goin' on!"

"Well, maybe nothing was. Maybe it was just a hug," said his friend Walter.

"Hell! What the hell she want a hug from him for? Have my arms dropped off?"

He thought that was a good answer, and so he said it again to Lucille. She said, "I've wondered about that myself."

He tried to talk to her about it and then he tried to fight with her about it but she wouldn't talk and she wouldn't fight. She told him there was nothing the matter but his dirty mind and his filthy lusts. It was her filthy lusts that he wanted to talk about, but she wouldn't admit she had any. It drove him crazy to be almost sure she was committing adultery and every time he tried to accuse her, because he was her husband and he had a right to, she acted as though he was the one who had done something wrong. "I'd forgive her," he said, "if I could just get the chance."

It preyed on his mind. Nobody had any sympathy for him. His friends didn't laugh in his face, but he could see they thought it was funny. And she had a way of getting people on her side. When he went to talk to his mother, she listened and was kind, but he found out Lucille had been there before him. "Honey, you should try not to give in to this awful jealousy," his mother said. "It'll break down a marriage quicker than anything in the world."

"But it ain't me! What she's..." He could not find words for his outrage. "What she's been doin'!" It was the best he could do.

"Now you don't know she's been doin' anything, son. You just think she has. And whatever you think, she's the woman God gave you and you have to find a way to be together like you promised in His sight you would. And," she added, "you just think of those sweet children of yours."

He went home that night desperate with longing. It was true, he did have a terrible lust, but it was not for flesh. What he craved was her remorse.

He hit her finally because he couldn't think what else to do. He didn't sock her, he didn't hit her with his fist; he always said he despised a man who would beat up on a woman. He just slapped her with his open hand. It took a second, less than a breath, less than a heartbeat. Later he explained that it would never have happened if she'd just been the least little bit sorry for what she'd done. But when he said she was like Jezebel, whose flesh was like dung on the field, when he told her that God had a place for whores and adulterers and if she didn't repent it would go hard with her on the Last Day, she didn't even answer. She just turned around and looked at him and shook her head. It was like she didn't even think it was worth answering him back. He couldn't think of anything to say to that look. He hit her harder than he meant to. "Hell," he said, "I never meant to hit her at all." Even so, it wouldn't have meant anything except for her stepping back, away from his hand. These things happen between couples. Only when she stepped back, the sole of her house shoe, that was a little bit loose, got caught up on the edge of the linoleum and she fell down onto the floor and on the way down she just hit her head on the corner of the range. It wasn't much. Everybody knows how much a cut on the head will bleed. They would have just washed it and forgot about it. Only the baby was in the doorway and she started to scream.

Lucille was sitting on the floor, moving her head slowly while blood ran into her eyes, and Jack didn't know who to pick up first. He went to Gracie, scared by her wide frightened eyes and her open mouth, sucking in air for her next scream. But before he reached her, Lucille had half stepped, half slid across to the child and gathered her up. She got to her feet awkwardly then, holding the baby, wobbling, unable to brace herself with her arms. Her blood was caught by Gracie's curls as the little girl lay her head against her mother's shoulder. She was quieter once Lucille had her, sobbing now, not shrilling frighteningly into the room any more. The blood was starting to stiffen around Lucille's cut. "That's a good sign," Jack thought. He went across, his arms out to hug them both and comfort them. He wasn't angry any more. He would forgive Lucille. He would wash both their faces and get a band-aid for Lucille's forehead. First thing tomorrow he would fix that linoleum. It was dangerous to have an edge that wasn't fast to the floor. But again, Lucille was quicker. She stepped back from him as though, he thought, he had raised his hand to her again, but she must know better.

"Keep away," she said. Her voice sounded strange and he realized that neither of them had spoken for a long time.

"Now…" he began. He took a step toward her.

"Keep away!" This time she shouted. The baby lifted her head and started to cry, turning her hot, wet face toward him. Lucille put her hand over Gracie's head and drew it back toward her breastbone. "Shh," she breathed softly, "Don't you be scared. Mama won't let him hurt my baby."

"Now...now you just stop that," he said. He couldn't work out what was going on. Why say that? She knew he'd never hurt a hair...

"I'm takin' Gracie into the bathroom," she said. "Don't you come."

"But you need me to help," he said.

She just looked at him and then she turned around and went out the door behind her.

He heard her walking through the living room and down the hall. It would have been quicker to go through the other door, but then she would have had to walk past him. He stood, listening to them. Running water, low voices. Gracie shouted, "No, no, no!" It was the favorite of her small collection of words. He could tell Lucille was trying to wash her hair. It was easier when he held her while Lucille poured the water over her head. He took a step toward the kitchen door and then stopped.

They didn't come back into the kitchen. Lucille put the baby into the buggy and pushed her out the back door without speaking to him. He waited for a while, listening for them to come back, and then he went out. It was time to pick the older ones up, Sandy from school and Johnny from kindergarten. She was upset and probably wouldn't remember, so he would do it. Then when he got them home, Lucille and Gracie would be back. They'd all have supper together and then he and Lucille would work everything out. This could turn out to be a good thing, he thought. Not a thing you would plan, but now that it had happened, it could be that they had turned a corner. He would be more careful from now on, and she would have learned that he meant what he said.

When he got to the Raggedy Ann and Andy Day Care, they told him that Johnny had already been picked up. "Was it his mom that come get him?" he asked. Miss Jean told him that yes, it was. He didn't like the way she looked at him. He wondered what Lucille had said. After that, he didn't expect Sandy would still be at school, but he went anyway. Gone. He stopped on his way home and bought a quart of rocky road ice cream. They weren't home when he got there.

He tracked them down finally. They weren't with her folks, which was the first place he'd tried, but they were at his mom and dad's. He had only tried them as a last resort; he wished he'd thought of it sooner, before he had phoned so many of their friends. It was embarrassing. When he asked for her, his mother said, "Honey, if I was you, I'd leave her alone tonight. You talk to her tomorrow and she might feel different."

"What do you mean, different? How does she feel now?"

"You call her up tomorrow."

He hung up. Never in his life before had he finished a conversation with his mother without saying goodbye and I love you, even when he was mad, even when he was drunk. Her "God bless..." was cut off by the click.

Then he did another thing he'd never done. Not just having a drink. He'd done that before, God knows. He'd got drunk often enough to make his mother tell his brother Dick to speak to him about it. And Dick had done that once or twice. But he'd never gone out of an evening with the intention in his mind of drinking until he couldn't drink any more. He'd fallen in with friends and had a second after his first and a skinful before morning, and sent himself home laughing at how crazy his feet were behaving. He'd never gone to seek out drink in a spirit of desperation before. He'd never seen himself as a skin curled around a kind of hole that couldn't be filled with anything but whisky.

That same night he met Sandra. The first thing he said to her when they were introduced was, "My little girl's got the same name as you," and she answered, "Well, I ain't no little girl, that's for sure."

He saw Sandra for a while, the same time he was meeting Lucille, explaining to her how that hadn't been the real him that night, telling her that if he could forgive her for what she'd been doing with Earl Sawyer, she ought to be able to forgive him for one smack. She'd put her hand to her head then, where she'd had two stitches. "But that was the stove that done that!" he said. It wasn't as if he'd taken a knife to her. And then she'd never admit that she'd done wrong with Earl, and that always made him mad, and all their conversations ended the same way, with her pretending to be afraid of him. After a while she moved out of his mom's house and back to their place, but by then she'd seen a lawyer and got them to say he had to move out of there.

He lodged with his friend Rob for a while, but they didn't really have room for him and he had to leave, finally. He always thought it would have been all right for him to stay if it had been up to Rob, but his wife didn't like him. He could have moved back in with his parents, and he did stay there for a week, but it didn't work out. He was always doing something wrong. Once Sandra came to pick him up in her car, for instance, and his dad treated her like she was some kind of a slut. So he moved into a room. It was easier. He kept his job and he gave most of his pay to Lucille for the kids. But she made it hard for him to see them. "It seems like I never can come when I want to," he said to Rob. "It seems like she's always got her own ideas. She's got to be right about ever'thing."

Later on he never could remember how he got into a fight that was bad enough to get him arrested. He knew he'd had a drink, but no more than usual. A man called Jake said something to him that made him mad and even though Jack gave him a chance to take it back, he wouldn't. It struck him funny, in a miserable way, that he couldn't remember what it was. It was something mean. Something insulting. He remembered telling him to take that back and Jake saying "Make me!" and then there was nothing either of them could do but fight. The police said afterward that he'd hit Jake with a chair, but he was sure he hadn't. Either somebody else had joined in and done it or Jake had just slammed into it by accident. He tried to explain but they were dead set on making him go to court. Then, instead of giving him a fine, the justice said he would have to go to trial. It wasn't going to be for disorderly conduct; they'd decided it was assault, even though Jake had started it. In view of his previous good character and his honorable discharge, they gave him bail, which his dad put up, and a date for his trial.

As the day got nearer and nearer, he became more and more sure that he could never get justice from the law. He left his father a letter to tell him that he would pay him back the bail money as soon as he could, and he left town without saying goodbye to anybody except Sandra. But he didn't say where he was going.

He stayed with his sister Sharon for a while in her nice house in Washington DC. It was good to see her again and he liked being Uncle Jack to her kids but she wouldn't stop arguing with him to go back. "You'll have to face the music one day," she said. After a while he couldn't stand it any more so he moved on.

He hadn't been at Dick's place an hour before Dick was on the phone to home. If he'd tell their mother where he was, why wouldn't he tell the police? He told him so. He called him a Judas.

"Does that make you Christ?" Dick asked. Jack hadn't ever heard that sound in his voice before. That sound of giving up on him, of not expecting anything.

"I wouldn't talk to a dog like you talk to me," he said.

"No," Dick said, "I expect you'd beat it to death."

Jack raised his hand. He didn't hit him, but he was ready to; he could have. He had raised his hand against him. "Thy brother's blood is crying out to Me from the ground." So he had to go. It was

the hardest parting yet. He felt as though he was leaving Dick and
God both.

†

He went on leaving places for twenty-five years. He had jobs and
left them or lost them; he went with some rough women and some
good ones who deserved better. He got married once. He knew
it was illegal. He always thought that one day he'd put it right—
get back in touch with Lucille and get a lawyer and a divorce and
then explain it to Margie and get married again. But he never got
around to it and after a while they split up anyway. So it was probably just as well. In all that time he went to church every so often,
but he never went up for the Lord's Supper.

It came to him one night while he was awake in the hospital
that he would soon be an old man and that he'd thrown his life
away. There was a storm outside the window and maybe it was that
made him think of the terrible storm in the Pacific. Had there been
a storm? He was sure he remembered lightning. He had been so
scared of dying that night, and he'd been so scared of hell. Here
he was now in the emergency ward where they'd found out his liver
was about shot and there was some kind of mess in his lung that
needed raking out. It came to him that if he had died that morning on Luzon, after he'd seen hell and the devil and found himself
under the loving arm of Jesus, it would have been better. But God
had spared him. For all this shit.

A nurse came to see what was wrong with him because he was
making a noise crying. "Now, what's the matter with you?" she
asked.

He said, "I wish I'd a died thirty year ago."

The nurse sat down next to him, smoothed his hair, wiped his
tears. "Oh now, you don't mean that," she said. "Everybody gets to
feeling miserable when they're sick. I expect you're missing your
folks."

When he went back to High Ridge after he was better, his mother
was dead. She'd been dead long years and he hadn't known. His
father said, "I wanted to tell you, but nobody knew where you'd
gone." Richard was old, unrecognizable, his wrists like chicken
bones, his eyes pale. He lived alone in the old house, but Dick
or his wife looked in on him most days. Dick still looked young.
He looked younger than Jack, and he looked like he'd done well.
"I'm awful glad to see you, Jack," he said, "I've been worried about
you." He talked as though he'd been away for a week or two, and

he never mentioned the last time they'd seen each other. Sharon was living in California. Her oldest was married out there. Lucille had remarried. Dick said that her husband was a good man, and he had treated her three just like his own. Lucille had divorced Jack in his absence after she'd met this new man, Samuel. Dick couldn't remember the year, but a ways back, he said. So maybe he had really been married to Margie after all. His children were grown up and they didn't remember him. Well, Gracie didn't, and Johnny just barely did. But they weren't very interested. Sandy lived in Charlotte, but it just happened she came back that weekend. She did sometimes. She remembered him.

When Jack said he wanted to go to church on Sunday, Dick said to come to his church. They brought their father with them. Richard didn't always go—it was too much of an effort—but he would this time.

And Sandy came. She sat at the back with her uncle and her grandfather. Toward the end of the service, she joined in singing the hymn of invitation. "Just as I am, Lord, without one plea," and watched Jack go up to the Mercy Seat to make his testimony.

Afterword

My experience of western North Carolina falls into three epochs. The first, extended but diffuse, was in my childhood. The second was the three years I spent there as an anthropologist, participating and observing with my husband and young family. Finally, in 2000, I took a plunge, short and intense, into the place to refresh my fieldwork and begin writing about it.

I was born in Washington DC, the first northern or the last southern city, depending on how you approach it. It was the city to which my father had come, in flight from small-town life in North Carolina, and my mother from the far west, in retreat from the Great Depression of the 1930s. Once he was away from the place that had stifled him when he was young, my father found a sentimental love for it. That is often the way with exiles. He never lived there again, but he never belonged to another place so thoroughly, and I was enveloped in his large family (he was one of eight children) during summers and fleeting visits at other times. I knew my numerous cousins. I suspect that my mother had no idea of the wonderful freedom we had there, the small-town, unsupervised right to roam. She would have been terrified at the use we made of it. I was never brave enough to walk along the railings of the railway bridge, but my cousin Harvey was, and how I admired him. We were let loose after breakfast to entertain ourselves in the wide world and came home when we got hungry. Nor is this just some artifact of an imagined 1950s innocence. My own children had very much the same liberty when my family lived there during my fieldwork twenty years later.

As a North Carolina child, I attended church and Sunday school (I never went near such a place at home), and I came back at the end of the summers I spent there with a southern accent, a store of Bible quotations, a taste for southern food, and other, less obvious, assimilations. As my father's daughter and, even more, as my grandparents' granddaughter, I was an insider.

When I lived in the hometown of my paternal relations, doing my first fieldwork, I was asked to identify myself by descent: "Now,

109

who was your daddy?" Even though I had a husband and three children by then, I was placed by whom I had come from. I was welcomed at once, as Manuel's daughter.

In fact I was from another place. I had grown up in Washington—after my parents parted when I was seven—with my northern mother. She was a westerner, really, not exactly a Yankee, but she was even more foreign by conviction than by origin. She was a principled, unshakeable atheist and she brought me up without what my North Carolina family was sure was the light of Christian truth. When I was with them, I was exposed to as much church as could possibly be provided (though it was no more than the home-reared children had), but it did not take. I reached and passed the age where I "should" have been baptized and never chose baptism. For much of my adolescence, one of my aunts sent me tracts urging me to accept Jesus as my Personal Savior. Later, I kept in touch with my southern family only sporadically. I was never estranged, but I was something of a stranger. For all our "shared bio-genetic substance," I had become an outsider—or, to borrow Lila Abu-Lughod's useful designation, an "insider-outsider."

Annette Khun writes in *Family Secrets* about her sense of recognition when she read Richard Hoggart's *The Uses of Literacy*. She and Hoggart, she said, were "both observers of something meaningful that we had left behind, if not quite lost. We shared the clarity of vision of the outsider who understands, because she or he has been there, what is being looked at and put into words...Hoggart's standpoint suggested I could salvage and put to good use what I had learned from living on both sides of the us/them divide." I, too, moved back and forth across that frontier.

†

If religion was one of the markers of my distance, it was also one of the aspects of southern life that exercised the strongest attraction, the greatest interest. Its influence is powerful, mysterious, and complicated.

In my childhood and on my every visit to North Carolina since, I have been aware of an intense religiosity there and of the way faith lives in the quotidian. I became accustomed to a pervasive resignation to the knowledge that the encroaching forces of secularism, of modernism, and of wickedness are sabotaging the effort of the faithful to build God's kingdom on earth.

Yet, though many people I knew devoted much of their time and energy to campaigning, arguing, or thinking about the increasing godlessness of the world, some felt it only peripherally and others, though churchgoers, were not very interested. Then, not everyone was a churchgoer. I knew people who did not go to church at all for one reason or another, many who attended out of habit, others who went and dismissed much of what they heard there but loved the singing, some who were openly skeptical, others who were faithful but troubled. Some people agonized openly about their eternal destination; others appeared never to doubt it. How to represent such diversity? "How can a whole people share a single subjectivity?" Vincent Crapanzano asked in 1986. The answer must be that it cannot. That *they* cannot. And no table is finely enough calibrated to represent the views, feelings, suspicions, sensitivities, and obsessions in even a small, even an apparently homogeneous community, complete with the intensities and distribution of those subjectivities. Milan Kundera has said of the novel what I believe to be true of the short story too, that its spirit is "the spirit of complexity. [It] says to the reader: 'Things are not as simple as you think.'"

†

Twenty five years ago, when I began to do fieldwork in Morganton, North Carolina, I was looking for data. I felt a responsibility to bring back from the field something harder, more countable, than stories. Yet complexity is resistant to hard data, and a story lay at the heart of every one of my interviews, conversations, and experiences in that place.

The short story form was always to hand, because the people among whom I lived and worked tell stories exuberantly and naturally. Everyday life is material for stories; you can hear them growing from simple morsels of information into rounded narratives in the course of a day. Then, like Jesus, people extract parables from mundane experience to serve instructive purposes. Churchgoers are urged to bear witness and to come forward to testify to the work the Lord has done in them; these witnessings and testimonies are stories, some told with drama and great skill. In church on one "Stewardship Sunday," I listened to a deacon relate how God had led him and his wife to tithe an amount calculated on their gross income when they had previously thought it would be enough to use the net figure. It sounds dry enough in précis, but it was a gripping story, and contained the memorable line, "All that dental work was just God's way of getting our attention."

I have a close interest in stories; I write stories of my own, and I have taught creative writing for most of my working life. My students, in common with other readers, writers, and critics, demand that a work be believable. Yet they know it is fiction; they want to believe it and not believe it at the same time. This is the same paradox that James Clifford touched on when he said that it is possible "to view good ethnographies as 'true fictions.'" But can stories represent what we like to call real life? Sometimes my writing students worry that, in making a story of an incident from their own experience, they are being untrue to it by changing it, taking it out of the realm of simple accuracy. I remind them that in fact, the changes have already taken place and have been taking place ever since whatever happened happened. Memory is an irresistible editor; it rearranges, shapes, corrects, sharpens, or smoothes events. By the time we say, "Here, let me tell you what happened..." we have already subjected random events to an editorial process that has given them form.

Ethnographers try to use field notes to pin memory firmly enough to keep it from slithering into untruth. The more rigorous the recording, the more accurate is the account, the more solid the basis for analysis and interpretation. But with every written word the reality of the text grows, the more it replaces the event it records. Simon Ottenberg writes of another set of notes the anthropologist carries away from the field, "the notes in my mind, the memories of my field research...my headnotes." The inevitable incongruence of the two sets of notes, the way that their outlines almost, but not quite, coincide, like the layers of color in a badly printed newspaper picture, is not so much a failure either of memory or of record keeping, as a representation of the ambiguity of the field experience.

"Unlike historians, anthropologists create their own documents," Roger Sanjec said in 1990. My stories are the documents I created, based upon notes, sound recordings, printed ephemera, and memories. In *Nuer Religion,* Evans-Pritchard uses a style of reporting that is somewhere between quotation and paraphrase; what he tells the reader about the *colwic* spirits, for instance, is his understanding of the Nuer's understanding of them. He creates a text upon which to build his interpretation. My created text is this collection of short stories.

Here is where they come from:

Jesus in America   *Lovely rhythm of language.*

Jesse, like all the people in the stories, is a made-up person. But in 2000 I did get to know a boy who had some of the qualities of his fictional representation: he was sweet natured and troubled, a little young for his age, and he had a conviction, at least for a while, that his destiny was to be a preacher of the gospel. His parents, like those in many of the families I knew, were in a sort of on-off relationship, and he lived in a family of strong, capable, nurturing women. He attended a Christian school at the cost of some sacrifice to his family.

The religious orientation and rules of behavior in "Christ the King School" have been reproduced with great fidelity from interviews I had with parents of children attending the town's Christian school, with two mothers who had sent their children (all of them sons) for a while before they decided it wasn't for them, and with the head teacher and the pastor and from their student handbook, "Working Together to Glorify God."

Cassie Bernall was one of the young people murdered in the Columbine High School massacre. A story began to circulate immediately after the atrocity that one of the gunmen (gunboys, really) asked her if she believed in God. She said yes and he shot her in the head, killing her instantly. The account of that final exchange was refuted very soon after, but the story survived. It is still possible to buy merchandise bearing the words "She Said Yes" or "Yes I Believe." A play based on the book of Cassie's life and death (*She Said Yes: The Unlikely Martyrdom of Cassie Bernall*) by Misty Bernall, her mother, was touring southern churches while I was there. I didn't attend, but I discussed it with a teenager who did, and I wrote in my notes, "I think he is a little envious of Cassie Bernall."

A Red Crayon

This one is the only one of my stories that seeks to imitate the voice in which I first heard it in the field. Although I have filled spaces in the narrative and added detail, the story of the woman who was alienated from institutional religion when she was a child and never found her way back is essentially the one I was told, leaning against the shelves in the secondhand bookshop, talking about God. The parallel story of the brutal brother-in-law was imported into this story from a conversation with another woman about her family. The two stories of justice from heavenly and earthly fathers, respectively, converged when I re-read and remembered them together.

The Mountains of Spices

When I was doing my first fieldwork in North Carolina, one of my white Baptist women friends had a seven-year-old daughter. They were a religious family and my friend, Kerrie, aspired to be the best person and the best Christian she could be. She told me that she was trying to raise her daughter free of the racism she had been brought up with. "I don't know," she said, "how I'll feel if she brings a colored boyfriend home one day. 'Course it may never happen, but if it does I'll have nobody but myself to blame. I've taught her to know no difference. But I don't know if I'd be ready for that." She thought. "It may never happen," she said.

Then, when the KKK staged a march down our high street, I asked one of the onlookers whether the Klan, who were merely a source of amusement that afternoon, had done anything destructive in the region in modern times. Several people remembered that a mixed couple (black man, white woman) had been threatened. Some men in Klan robes—nobody knew who they were or where they were from—had burned a cross in the young man's front yard. When I asked what had become of the couple, I was told that they had gone to California. I took that as code for "as far away as they could get."

I made Kerrie's daughter into Ruth and imagined Kerrie's dread come true twenty years on, so as to consider those liberal-minded, moral southerners who know that racism has outlived its time but who cannot, in the moment of test, let it go. The line I give to the woman in the shop, "I don't care how much you think you love him, I don't see how anybody could do such a thing to her mother," is a close paraphrase of what I was told by an elderly woman relating an ancient scandal in her own family. I spoke to several people (all but one of them black) who had a relative who had married outside his or her own race. All the mixed-race couples had moved away.

Personal Storage

This is the most complicated of my stories, but it has the most straightforward genesis. The Sunday school class is as close to the real one as I could make it; the visitor/narrator is like me in intent and attention; and the prayers, the appeal, the scripture reading, the didactic play, and the Farm Home Administration story are all based on real experience. The narrator's imaginings are purely my own imaginings and are meant to make explicit the role of narrative in religious life. They expose the narrator's addiction to story making, too.

I meant Martha's obsessive hoarding to bear some symbolic weight, as well. Commentators from Mark Twain in the nineteenth century to W. J. Cash in the mid-twentieth, to Joan Didion in the twenty-first have remarked on the southern propensity to make the past its treasure; to hold onto it when it would be more profitable to let it go.

A Moment of Rapture

Not all those who say they expect the end of the world to come according to the chiliastic schedule in The Book of Revelation believe it with exactly the same type and quality of belief. And not all those who await Apocalypse and Armageddon think the Rapture will precede it, to spare them the time of Tribulation. But there are those who do sincerely believe that when the earth has run its troubled course and the end time has come, Christ will come again, not, this time, as a helpless baby, but as a conqueror and that he will scoop up his own, saved people (there will not be very many of them) into heaven, leaving the others to face the war, pestilence, fire, and famine the Bible has promised before the final, conclusive battle between the forces of good and those of evil. Because the saved will be taken up "in the twinkling of an eye," the cars they are driving, the planes they are piloting, the surgical operations they are doing, will all be left uncontrolled. There is very little in the Bible to support belief about the Rapture, and it has always been a minority belief amongst Christians. The very sparseness of biblical description seems to have encouraged an (almost un-fundamentalist) creativity among those who do believe. The sticker that reads, "During the Rapture This Car Will Be Driverless" is sometimes affixed to the car bumper in a spirit of playfulness, but for some, the playfulness exists alongside profound belief.

Laurel, in my story, believes in the truth and imminent reality of the Rapture. What she does not believe in, despite her devotion, is the security of her own salvation. Laurel is made up of course, but her story was told me as a true one, from the barking dogs to the final discovery of the innocent child who could not possibly have been left behind.

Jack at the Mercy Seat

It is possible to join a Baptist church in North Carolina by presenting a letter of transfer from your "home church," by testifying to your acceptance of Jesus and being baptized, or by returning to your earlier faith with a testimony of God's work in your life and renewing your promises. The "mercy seat" appears in the Bible's description of the temple in Jerusalem as the space between the wings of the golden cherubs on either side of the altar; in Baptist churches the phrase is used for the place, both physical (at the front of the church, often by the Lord's Supper table) and spiritual, where confession, forgiveness, and acceptance occur. One Sunday, when the hymn of invitation was played, an elderly man made his way up the aisle to stand before the congregation, and said this:

> I want to take a few moments for a testimony to this church and to the three members of my family who are with me. As I speak you will understand why they are not up here with me. We have had such glorious preaching this morning. Your minister. His preaching was just irresistible to me. How could anyone listen to such preaching and not accept Jesus, not only as savior, but as Lord. Now Jesus has been my savior since New Year's night in 1945, but he has not always been my lord. In 1945 I came to Jesus because I was in fear for my life and I was in fear of hell. I thought I might have to face my God in the nearest hour. I was not living right, and I knew better. I was raised in a Christian home and I knew that the only way to save my soul and my eternal life was to make Jesus my savior. For that is the offer he has made to us and on that night, when I had been trying to forget my fear with drinking and enjoying myself, I knew in my heart it would never work that way, and the only way I could have blessed security was to take him up on that offer. And I praise Him for putting that knowledge into my heart that night.
>
> But much as I said I loved the Lord Jesus, I took his precious gift of salvation and I did not thank him with my life. After just a little while, I was being unfaithful to all the promises I made that night. I can't blame anybody else, because I had been told that if Jesus is your savior, then he has to be your lord also. Once you accept Him, then you don't belong to yourself any more, but you belong to Him. He is your savior and your redeemer because He has bought you with a price. You are His bondslave and a slave doesn't have any rights. I was told it, but I was not truly convicted in my heart. But I went on all these years and behaved as if I had no lord. I was saved, but I wasn't in the center of God's will for me. And when the blessed opportunity came for me to help another precious soul, I was so sunk in my own sin and my own

pride that I could not share the gift of my salvation and all I offered was blame. Now I can't hardly forgive myself for missing that blessed opportunity, but I know that God will forgive me, for his precious Son's sake.

So now I am rededicating my life to him. We have to know who we are in this life and we have to know whose we are. And we are called upon to speak the truth in love. I have been defeated spiritually in my own life because I spoke the truth in anger. But God does not accept defeat and Jesus Christ will not accept defeat, for He has won the victory for us on the cross. And I thank your minister and I thank you all and I thank the ones that has prayed for me these long years and I thank my Savior and my Lord for bringing me to this place on this Lord's Day.

All the elements for "Jack at the Mercy Seat" appear in this testimony, which I kept as a field note; I made the story by inventing what in Jack's speech was left mysterious or incomplete: his family, his failure to forgive, the circumstances of his early conversion, his return.

I don't usually research the background for short stories, but Jack, who had left so much out, had been meticulous about the date of his encounter with Jesus, as the born again often are, and I looked to see what was going on in the war then (he looked the right age to have been a young soldier at that time). I chose to look at the Pacific theater because that's where my father served, and because Americans were deployed there so late in the war. I discovered that the big offence on Leyte (coincidentally, my dad was stationed there) was launched on January 1, 1945, and that one of the troop carriers in service had been damaged in one of the first kamikaze raids, which had come at the end of the previous November, with 19 killed and 72 wounded. It was rebuilt in record time and relaunched before the new year. So I was able to bracket Jack's awakening between Thanksgiving and New Year's, those great American occasions for national joy, and to give his vision of hell a this-worldly context.

†

At first, I meant for the stories to be no more than a kind of elaborated version of my field notes, a way of making available to the reader the text that I made from my research and with which I was thinking about the lived religious life in an environment of fundamentalist belief. But in the course of writing them down, they became stories for their own sake. For the pleasure of the telling them.

They are also an attempt to do justice to the people among whom I worked, who can be reduced to nothing less complicated than their stories. Anthropologists often refer to the people in their research area as "my people." I claim those in North Carolina as my people in a way that implicates my past as well as my curiosity.

It has been suggested to me that the next time I do research, I should choose people I am not so fond of. These stories are, whatever else they turn out to be, a record of my time among people the insider in me was—mostly—fond of and of a religious life that was sometimes outlandish to the outsider in me, but one that is lived with passionate sincerity.

Bibliography

Abu-Lughod, Lila. *Writing Women's Worlds: Bedouin Stories.* Berkeley: University of California Press, 1993.

Cash, W.J. *The Mind of the South.* London: Thames and Hudson, 1971.

Charmaz, Kathy and Richard G. Mitchell, Jr. "The Myth of Silent Authorship: Self, Substance and Style in Ethnographic Writing." In *Reflexivity and Voice,* edited by Rosanna Hertz. Thousand Oaks: Sage, 1997.

Clifford, James. "Partial Truths." In *Writing Culture: The Poetics and Politics of Ethnography,* edited by James Clifford and George E. Marcus. Berkeley: University of California Press, 1986.

Crapanzano, Vincent. "Hermes Dilemma: the masking of Subversion in Ethnographic Description." In *Writing Culture: The Poetics and Politics of Ethnography,* edited by James Clifford and George E. Marcus. Berkeley: University of California Press, 1986.

Didion, Joan. "Mr Bush and the Divine." *The New York Review of Books.* November 20, 2003.

Evans-Pritchard, E.E. *Nuer Religion.* Oxford: Oxford University Press, 1956.

Kuhn, Annette. *Family Secrets: Acts of Memory and Imagination.* London: Verso, 1995.

Kundera, Milan. *The Art of the Novel.* London: Faber and Faber, 1990.

LaHaye, Tim and Jenkins, Jerry B. *Left Behind.* Wheaton, Illinois: Tyndale House Publishers, 1995.

Ottenberg, Simon. "Thirty Years of Fieldnotes: Changing Relationships to the Text." In *Fieldnotes: The Makings of Anthropology,* edited by Roger Sanjek. Ithaca and London: Cornell University Press, 1990.

Twain, Mark. *Life on the Mississippi.* New York and London: Harper and Brothers, 1902.